THE GIRL WHO GOT AWAY

JACK MCSPORRAN

J.A. LEAKE

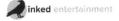

ALSO BY THE AUTHORS

Co-written Novels

I Know You Killed Them (forthcoming)

Talking to Strangers (forthcoming)

Also by J.A. Leake:

The Lies Between Us

Also by Jack McSporran:

Dead Awake

The Maggie Black Series:

- *Vendetta*

- *The Witness*

- *The Defector*

- *Kill Order*

- *Hit List*

- *Payback*

- *Origin (forthcoming)*

In loving memory of my grandfather, Bill.
- Jack

For all the mental health professionals I've worked with over the years, who have dedicated their lives to helping those struggling with PTSD.
- J.A.

1

THEN

The sudden roar of a diesel engine was monstrous in its intensity, easily drowning out the *drip, drip, drip* of a leaky pipe.

In the dark, damp basement, Erin Lewis had never heard a more welcome sound. She scrambled to her feet and listened hard, heart throbbing in her ears. The engine sound faded as though the vehicle was being driven away, and her eyes immediately darted to the grimy window. In her darkest moments, she had believed he would never leave, and now that he had, she stood momentarily frozen. Escaping this basement had been all she'd thought about, but now that the opportunity was here, terror filled her at the thought of failing.

She hadn't worked this hard to let fear stop her, though.

Chips of paint littered the floor beneath the window, where Erin had scraped the frame free with a broken screwdriver, and at times her own nails, which were now ragged and bloody.

She moved silently over to the window and inched it open, wincing at its groaning protest. Her muscles strained, but the window gave way. Fresh, humid air poured in, and Erin breathed it like she was surfacing from deep underwater.

Her body shook from the rush of adrenaline, and her ears strained for even the tiniest whisper of sound. If she didn't escape now, there'd never be another chance.

Now, she thought. *It has to be now.*

Erin's breath rushed out, so forcefully she was sure she'd be discovered. She squeezed through the slim basement window, biting back a whimper when her hips got stuck. She wrenched free and scrambled to her feet. Deep scratches stung her thighs from the window frame, and she took great gulps of fresh air.

The open lawn, riddled with weeds and fallen tree branches lay in front of her. Her eyes darted to the woods beyond, where she would be hidden amongst the trees and thick undergrowth. She'd always been afraid of the woods, of the things with fur and teeth and claws, but she knew now there are worse things. The woods would be her sanctuary. Only first she must race across the open yard.

She risked one more glance at the house, the ugly hulking thing that had become part of her nightmares. The house was a malevolent face watching her, the dark windows the eyes, and the front door with its collapsing steps a gaping mouth. Her body quivered in anticipation of the mad dash to the woods, but terror kept her legs from moving. Any second she expected a hand with dirty fingernails to grab her and drag her back. The smell of an unwashed body and cigarettes nearly kept her from running, and for one terrible moment she thought he had come back early. But the stench was coming from her.

And then, as if a pistol had been fired, she shot off. She hardly felt the grass on her bare feet, and then it gave way to leaves and pine needles as she crashed into the woods. If there were animals making noises now, she couldn't hear them over the pounding of her heart and her explosive breaths. The wind whipped her tangled hair back, and although it was cooler in the dark of night, it didn't have the bite of winter yet. She didn't know where to go, but she'd rather die out here, free in the woods, than spend another second in that house.

Branches tore at her hair and shirt as she ran, like

jagged fingernails grabbing at her, trying to pull her back into the basement. She'd never been a runner, and her lungs burned. They joined her bone-deep exhaustion and pain in almost every part of her body until she got so weak she stumbled over a root and crashed to the ground. For a moment, she lay there dazed. Her bruised and battered body begged for her to stop. To close her eyes and drift off to sleep. To give up.

Only the fear of *him* coming for her made her stumble back to her feet. Her body screaming in protest, she pushed herself up and continued in a limping half-jog.

Moonlight slipped through the gnarled branches of the trees that loomed over her. Distorted shapes stretched across the little light it provided and Erin tried not to dwell on what could be lurking in the shadows. She didn't know where to go. Her only goal was to put as much distance between her and that monstrous house as she could. What if this was just a dream? What if she was still trapped there? Every step she took felt like she was walking underwater. It made it hard to tell reality from a nightmare. Her bare feet slipped on an upturned root, and she cried out as something sharp pierced the sensitive skin.

I can't be dreaming then, she thought, even as her mind jumped to the next fear. Could she find her way out of the woods?

She didn't know, but she had to try. She pushed on for hours, until the moon slipped lower in the sky. The woods grew ever darker.

And then, when she thought she couldn't go on, the woods thinned. She caught sight of something gray snaking through the trees. She came to a stumbling stop and stared hard, trying to make sense of what she was seeing. It dawned on her slowly, and then tears pricked her eyes. A road. She found the road.

She squeezed the last drops of energy from her body and pushed herself into a run.

The trees and undergrowth tried to snatch her back, but she burst free. The rough road and tiny rocks tore into her bare feet as she limped along. She wasn't sure where she was, but she thought it might be the road into town. The one she'd been taken from days ago. The memory of it threatened to cripple her, but she pushed it away. She had to keep going. She had to find help.

After several minutes of painful limping, she heard the gentle rumbling of an engine in the distance. Icy fingers of fear traced down her spine. Was it him? Had he found her?

She glanced to her left, where the shadowy woods lay. She could go there now and hide, but she might miss her chance for someone to pick her up and take her to the police. Bouncing from foot to foot, she warred with herself.

The engine sound grew louder, and she could see headlights in the distance. She listened hard. It wasn't the roar of the diesel engine.

The tears turned into feral-sounding sobs as she stood as close to the road as she dared and waved her arms. The old, beat-up pickup truck slowed and came to a jolting stop when the driver noticed her. Erin hurried over to the passenger side and yanked the door open.

The man had a thick beard and kind eyes. "Are you all right?" he asked.

Erin choked on a sob. All right? She'd never be all right again.

2

NOW

Cool, crisp air swept over Erin Masters's face as she stepped out of her hired car and onto the busy New York sidewalk. A slight smile touched her lips as she headed toward the glass and steel high rise building. She loved autumn in the city. It wasn't terribly hot, the sewers didn't stink as much, and best of all, it was the anniversary of when she'd started her own PR firm.

Emblazoned in gold above the entrance was Masters PR, and she never got tired of seeing it. She pulled open the door and walked into the lobby. Inside was all clean, modern lines and walls of glass that let in as much of the New York City sun as possible.

With her designer sunglasses still on, she strode across the floor, high heels making a satisfying tone on the marble. When she got to the elevator, she pressed the call button without hesitation, as though she hadn't a care in the world.

The truth was, though, that already her insides quivered and roiled like a mass of snakes.

The door opened, and she stepped into the elevator. A well-groomed man in a dark suit hurried to make it inside with her, and for a moment, her finger hovered over the close door button. He stepped over the threshold just in time, flashing a relieved smile at her, but she couldn't bring herself to return it. She moved to the back of the elevator and let him press the floor he needed.

The door swished shut, and Erin's stomach bottomed out. Instantly she was transported back in time to a small, dark basement room. The nauseating scent of must and mildew filled her nose, and a chill raced up her spine. With one hand, she reached out and touched the striped wallpaper of the elevator. Dr. Suarez told her it would ground her in the present moment and remind her that she was in the here and now—not trapped in a torturous basement thirteen years ago. Erin still tried it every time she was in an elevator, but it never completely took away the feeling of terror. Of course, her sessions with that particular doctor had been over seven years ago, and Erin hadn't been back. She had a new therapist now, Dr. Monterey, who knew not to bother wasting her time with psycho-analysis. Any time she did, Erin shut her down.

The elevator took forever, just like it did every day. She avoided eye contact with the man, keeping her eyes closed altogether behind her sunglasses. He got off at the fifteenth floor, but she was going to the top. When the doors swished shut again, she was alone. Her lungs compressed until she saw black spots in her vision. Panic set in—her chest felt like an elephant was sitting on it. She was trapped here and would never get out. What if she passed out this time? What if the elevator doors opened, and all her staff found her crumpled on the floor? She wouldn't be able to survive the humiliation of it. She couldn't *breathe.*

Ten more seconds, she knew. She counted them slowly in her mind as sweat poured down her. "I'm in an elevator, not a basement," she said out loud. Her heart continued to pound like it didn't believe her.

Just before the door opened again, she took out the tissue she kept exactly for this purpose, blotted the sweat beading at her hairline, and quickly spritzed her face with a makeup setter. At least she didn't have to worry about underarm sweat anymore—not since she switched to a clinical-strength antiperspirant.

When the door finally opened, she stepped out

onto the twentieth floor, legs shaky and weak. She swallowed down her terror and rearranged her face into its typical mask of confidence and ease. Inside, adrenaline raced through her like she'd just fought for her life. To counter her trembling hands, she gripped her leather bag tightly in her fist. She never signed anything in front of anyone first thing in the morning—her hand would shake too badly for her to even write her name.

She walked past other offices until she reached her own, decorated with the modern opulence her clients had come to expect. Erin had quickly learned that if you wanted to be taken seriously in this city, you sure as hell better act the part. And her clients expected a flashy, modern PR company with an office to match. This space delivered with floor-to-ceiling glass windows that let in enough natural light to make the white shelves and desks look almost ethereal. The furniture was an eclectic mix of styles, in bright colors with rich fabrics. Modern, bright lighting chased away any trace of shadow in the place—this was Erin's sanctuary.

When Erin neared her own office, Nikki, her personal assistant for the past five years, fell into step beside her. She was much taller than Erin—almost six feet—so she had to adjust her strides to match. Her dark, tight curls were piled high on top of her head, and she was dressed in her usual button-down, pencil skirt, and heels combo that made her look like a sexy librarian. She pulled her tablet out with Erin's itinerary for the day.

"Okay, meeting at nine," she said, scrolling through her spreadsheet, nails painted a bright red, "followed by a phone call with Westinghouse at eleven, and I've got your lunch down from twelve thirty to two."

"You can strike lunch from my schedule," Erin said with a wave as she reached the door of her office. "It'll just be a working lunch at my desk. I've got a lot to follow up on today."

Nikki huffed. "That just means you'll drink two shots of espresso and skip eating altogether. I'm trying to look out for your health here. Last thing we need is you getting sick. You need to drink green tea and elderberry at the very least."

Nikki was completely into holistic health, and Erin wasn't into taking care of herself at all, beyond the fact that she refused to ever drink or smoke. Remembering to eat regular meals and drink enough water often escaped her attention. She had far too many other things to focus on.

"I'll get right on that," Erin tossed over her shoulder as she walked into her office.

Nikki muttered something under her breath and then said, "I'll bring you a sandwich later."

A smile played on Erin's lips as Nikki closed the door behind her. Nikki didn't take no for an answer, which was exactly why Erin hired her in the first place.

She was a girl just out of school, and when Erin asked about previous experience, she'd brazenly said, "None at all. But you can count on me to work crazy long hours, take reduced pay until your business gets off the ground, and help chase down clients to add to your roster."

Erin had thanked her for the interview and sent her on her way, but Nikki called her every day asking if the job was still available and reminding her that there was no one who'd work as cheap as she would. After a week, she'd worn Erin down and won the job, though she probably regretted it that first year. It was hell just starting out, but Erin always knew she'd make it to the top.

Now Erin couldn't imagine the place without Nikki. She handled all the tedious organizational stuff so Erin was free to do what she really loved: head hunting clients from her competitors and looking out for new and financially fruitful opportunities for her current ones. Nothing made this easier than social media.

She turned on her computer and pulled up all the major sites, scanning for news, trends, and memes related to the fashion industry. At the same time, she had a notes document up, ready to brainstorm PR opportunities.

She found what she was looking for on Instagram. An influencer named Zoe with over two million followers had built up her fashion platform entirely around pajamas. She made them look sexy, fun, and utterly desirable. Zoe was perfect for one of Erin's new clients, the Happy in Plaid brand, since they were in the business of flannel, and that included a whole line of pjs and slippers in fun prints.

Erin immediately shared Zoe's account with Nikki. *I need her for the HP project.*

On it, Nikki texted back. *What's her incentive package?*

All the pajama-related flannel her little heart desires. We can pay the standard rate, too, but see how she feels about the free stuff first.

Nikki responded with a simple thumbs-up emoji, and Erin checked it off her mental list for now. She knew Nikki would handle everything and get Zoe on board by the end of the day. It was what Nikki did best.

The rest of the day flew by in a frenzy of fast-paced work, in the way only a PR firm can. Erin loved every second of it because it kept her mind busy. She couldn't dwell on anxious thoughts or worries when she was on the phone or in a meeting without breaks.

When Erin finally took a moment just to go to the restroom, Nikki hurried to her side. "Christopher Roland is on the phone for you. Says it's urgent."

Erin groaned. "Urgent to him could mean that his goldfish died."

"I think it was an eel," she said with a crooked

smile, "but yeah, he doesn't seem to fully grasp what a PR firm does."

Resigned, Erin went to her desk and picked up the phone. "Christopher? This is Erin. What can I do for you?"

"Oh, thank God, Erin. Finally someone with sense. It's an emergency."

Erin's teeth clenched at the insinuation that Nikki had no sense, since she was the one who had already tried to deal with his emergency. She forced her face to relax—clients could sense when she was annoyed. "I'm here to help. What's going on?"

"I have been informed that some little basic bitch posted on Insta that my clothes are cheap."

Erin raised her eyebrows. Depending on how influential the poster was, this could be a genuine concern. Christopher Roland's couture brand had just launched in the States, and the last thing they needed was for it to be torn apart on social media. "I can see why you're upset. Do you have the person's handle?"

"It's Bev Little," he said, voice full of contempt.

Erin typed the name into Instagram and frowned as countless accounts came up. She clicked on the first few but none seemed like a huge fashion influencer. When she clicked on the third name from the top, it showed a girl holding up one of Christopher's more unusual designs—a skin-tight black dress with a full neckline of feathers—with her nose wrinkled in distaste. Erin immediately understood what had made Christopher so upset, but as she opened her mouth to tell him so, she looked at the girl's follower numbers and almost laughed.

"I can definitely see why this upset you, Christopher," she said, but before she could continue, he immediately launched into a screaming tirade where he insulted everything from the girl's hair (fried) to her nails (disastrous) to her place of birth (backwater town).

"How did she even get a hold of that dress?" he demanded, scarcely drawing breath. "It's straight off the runway!"

"And we can look into that, but what I want you to understand is that this account isn't anywhere near influencer size. She only has a few thousand followers."

"That's thousands too many!"

Erin was glad they weren't on a video call. It left her eyes free to roll with impunity. "I hear you. I know it's frustrating to see a design you worked hard on treated like that, but to put her numbers in perspective, we only promote our clients with fashion influencers who have *at least* a million followers."

"It still shows up in the hashtag," he said, but he didn't sound nearly as incensed.

"It does, but the fact that she's holding the dress is a good thing. It means people will see it, even if she's making a face. Doesn't matter. It will still get the word out about your brand."

"I still want it taken down," he grumbled.

"I think that would be a waste of your time and effort, honestly. We currently have a slew of elite models, actresses, and influencers—amassing over one hundred million users—preparing to launch some gorgeous shots of your dresses. This picture can't even compare, and even if it could, she doesn't have enough followers to share it. In fact," Erin said, looking at the post's details again, "this was posted last night, and she's only had about ten comments on it and a little over fifty likes. Influencers typically get tens of thousands of likes and hundreds of comments."

"I still think someone should tell her that is *not* how you treat a couture dress."

"It's a gorgeous dress," Erin said, striving for a sympathetic tone even though she thought it looked like the girl was holding up a dead buzzard. "You could have your assistant do some investigating to see if this Bev Little has connections to someone in the fashion world, but if it was me, I wouldn't waste another second of your precious time on it. You're getting ready for New York Fashion Week, right?"

"Ugh, yes. It's been a stress-fest nightmare."

"We all turn to social media as a distraction when we're stressed, but you should be happy this isn't a PR concern. Just concentrate on your gorgeous designs, and we'll handle everything else, okay?"

Christopher let out a huge sigh. "Yes, you're right,

Erin. Thanks for figuring this all out for me. I feel like a new man...ready to tackle my designs again."

"Of course. Let me know if you need anything else. I'm always available for my best clients."

They said their good-byes and Erin checked her phone. It was already time to leave for the day. She thought of a ride in the elevator, and her stomach immediately tensed.

Later, she thought. She'd leave later. For now, there was always more work to do.

By the time Erin arrived home, it was well past dinnertime. She'd ended up scarfing down the vegetarian sandwich Nikki had brought her around four, so she wasn't even hungry yet. She never could eat as soon as she got home anyway. Not after enduring another panic attack on the elevator. She'd taken the stairs today instead—at least it was easier going down all those flights than up.

After double-checking that the door was firmly locked behind her, she crossed over to the space that served as her bedroom, where her bed rested against the exposed brick. She took a moment to survey her open-concept apartment. She'd specifically sought out this type of living space a few years ago when she'd first upgraded to living in Manhattan. It wasn't that she could only afford a studio apartment in NYC—in fact, this apartment was bigger than her family house in West Virginia—no, she couldn't stand for there to be any dark corners in her home. She wanted to be able to know for sure that she was alone—that no one was hiding without her knowing.

She went around and turned on all the lights to banish the gloom, and then she changed into her workout gear of skin-tight leggings, sports bra, and fluorescent running shoes. She tied her long hair back into a ponytail before climbing onto her state-of-the-art stationary bike. It had a screen that allowed her to virtually ride up and down mountain trails without ever having to leave her apartment.

Once, Erin had belonged to a gym. She attended spinning classes and took advantage of the extensive weight room. But one day a man came over and asked for her number. Objectively, he was extremely attractive. His body was lean and muscular, his eyes were a gentle brown, and his smile was kind. Even his personality seemed amiable. While a lot of men she met in the city were overconfident to the point that they became pushy and rude, he at least spent some time trying to warm her up with small talk. But when he stepped closer to her, she could smell the faintest whiff of cigarettes beneath his sweat. She hadn't even responded—she'd just backed away from the man like he was a serial killer and fled the gym. She never went back.

Now, she cycled alone and let the endorphins chase away the shaky, tangled mass of snakes that took up residence in her belly the moment she stepped into the closed space of the elevator. She rode for a full hour, until her legs were like jelly when she finally got off.

After a hot shower, she ate leftover Chinese food while scrolling idly through social media. When a news article came up in her feed discussing a minor robbery that had happened in West Virginia, her finger paused.

Memories of her hometown threatened to overtake her—she hadn't been back since she left home at eighteen. These thoughts reminded her of her baby sister, though, and guilt churned darkly in her stomach. Brooke was a junior in high school now, but Erin hadn't seen her since she was a little girl. Horribly, she'd left Brooke behind when she'd made her escape. She'd been eighteen and desperate to get the hell out of there, and she couldn't have taken care of her sister any better than their alcoholic mother could.

Erin never let herself do this, but she pulled up Brooke's Instagram page. It was filled with selfies of her with friends, of parties and football games, of kisses shared with a boyfriend. In every shot she was smiling or laughing, cheeks glowing. But Erin knew just because the pictures looked happy didn't mean that was how Brooke's life was behind closed doors.

She kept scrolling through the photos, but when she came to an old one of Brooke and their mother, she clicked out of Instagram as fast she could.

It was too late though. A memory broke free before Erin could suppress it again: *Mama, something horrible happened to me.*

Now, she threw her phone down on her bed and got up to make some tea. She wouldn't let her mind go down that path. That was a long time ago, and she was a totally different person. Wealthy and successful. Someone who wasn't held back by her past—she'd risen above it.

But as the night progressed, Erin's mind couldn't hold out against the onslaught of memories. They assaulted her senses. The smell of mildew and iron, the feel of damp cold, the insidious sound of a shoe scraping on wooden stairs, and worst of all: the shadowy darkness that threatened to swallow her up.

It was clear a little cup of tea wasn't going to work to help her go to sleep, so she reached for the bottle of pills in her nightstand drawer. The bottle was much lighter than it should've been when she lifted it up.

She cursed herself when she shook out the last pill into her hand. One wouldn't even take the edge off the monstrous specter that was her anxiety. Why had she taken so many the night before? Her backup bottle was all the way in her desk at work. There was no way in hell she'd make it there without some sort of breakdown.

Grabbing her phone, she checked her calendar for the next appointment with Dr. Monterey. She nearly whimpered in relief when she saw it was for tomorrow morning.

But first she'd have to get through the night.

Erin left the lamp beside her bed on. She couldn't bear to sleep in the darkness. Not again.

3

The next morning, before work, Erin hurried up the steps of the elegant brownstone on the Upper West Side. Her neck prickled like someone was watching her, and she tried not to look fearfully over her shoulder. The chances of being attacked here in this wealthy, upscale part of the city were practically nonexistent, but it didn't stop her heart from pounding or her palms from sweating. Like the elevator, Erin had learned to work *around* her fears. She sure as hell hadn't been good at working through them.

Her phone rang from her bag, and she jumped at the sound. With a huff of irritation, she pulled it out and checked the caller ID. An unknown number flashed across the screen, and her phone identified it as coming from West Virginia.

She physically recoiled from the phone and hit the

decline call button. Then she blocked the caller for good measure before finally pulling open the door to Dr. Monterey's office. A call from someone in West Virginia was the last thing she needed to deal with when she was out of her meds.

Once inside, she tried to slow her breathing so she wasn't huffing and puffing like she'd just run all the way there. She went into the first room on the right, which had been converted into a comfortable waiting room with plush couches and armchairs facing a marble fireplace. No one else was there since Erin was usually the first client of the day. She jiggled her leg while she waited for Dr. Monterey. Her anxiety was always ten times worse when she dealt with insomnia. She was no stranger to sleepless nights, but her body always made sure she paid the price the next day. Nikki had accused her once of staying out and partying too hard, but that was giving Erin's social life too much credit. She couldn't admit the lame truth—that memories of something that happened a million years ago still kept her up at night—so she just stared Nikki down until she dropped it.

Another minute, and her therapist emerged from the adjoining room. Dr. Monterey was petite, with dark hair shot with gray. She wore it pulled back in a severe bun that looked painful. Erin wondered if she did it to smooth some of the wrinkles on her face because it seemed to pull her skin taut. She wore large cat-eye glasses and always dressed in fitted black dresses with sensible pumps.

"Erin, you may come in now," she said with a cool smile.

Erin took her usual leather armchair across from Dr. Monterey. On a small table beside her therapist was a prescription pad, notepad, and expensive-looking fountain pen. Erin only cared about one of these things, and it grated on her nerves that she had to do this song and dance with her therapist every time before she could get it.

"How are you?" Dr. Monterey asked after taking her seat across from Erin.

"Fine. Busy." Erin's leg started jiggling again, and she saw the therapist's eyes jump to it. With effort, she made herself stop.

"Work has been busy?"

"Yes, but busy is good. Busy means we have plenty of clients."

She nodded thoughtfully. "And what about your personal life? Has that been busy too?"

Erin let out a self-deprecating laugh. "I don't have time for a personal life." Her leg started juggling up and down again.

"Hm, so you've said. I don't mean this in a rude way, Erin, but you don't look so good today. Did you have a nightmare again?"

Erin stiffened, thinking of her sleepless night, of

the nightmares she couldn't escape. She dreamed of her time down in the basement, of what he did to her.

"Do you want to talk about it?"

"No," Erin snapped, her eyes narrowed. "I don't. I don't want to talk at all. I want to get my prescription and get out of here, same as every other month."

Dr. Monterey frowned, the gesture pulling her bun even tighter. "You won't ever make progress toward letting go of your traumatic past if you don't talk about it. The nightmares will continue, and you won't ever be able to move on. You'll just be stuck there, never really free."

Erin sat up straighter. "I'm the CEO of my own damn company. I'd say I've done pretty well at 'moving on.'"

"Your professional life has flourished, it's true. But what about your nonexistent personal life? What about the nightmares and the panic attacks?" She gave Erin a pointed look. "Do you still practically have a breakdown whenever you ride on an elevator?"

Erin smiled without humor. "That's what the Xanax is for."

It was why she went to Dr. Monterey. Most psychiatrists didn't want to prescribe the old-school drug that was known for its addictive qualities. They preferred antidepressants and mood stabilizers. She didn't need that. She needed a drug that helped her forget, that turned her fear into apathy.

"Taking the Xanax will never help you overcome this, Erin. You'll still be trapped in that basement, like you never escaped. You're letting him win because he still has a hold on your life, despite all your success."

Erin stood, her hand on her pounding head. "Enough with the psychoanalysis. I'm only here for my refill." When Dr. Monterey heaved a sigh and grabbed her prescription pad, Erin added, "You could see me even less if you'd write it for a ninety-day supply."

She shook her head. "You know I can't do that."

Erin reached inside her bag and pulled out her wallet. She withdrew a few hundreds. "Just a few extra then. To get me through to our next session."

Dr. Monterey hesitated for only a moment before holding out her hand. Erin handed her the bills, and the therapist retrieved a small bottle from her pocket.

"Thank you," Erin said as Dr. Monterey handed over the prescription and extra bottle of pills. She knew the therapist would give in. She always did. The psychoanalysis she tried at the beginning of every session was clearly just to assuage her guilt over prescribing the Xanax. Erin wished she'd just drop the pretense and let her come and get her prescription and leave.

"I'll see you in a month," Dr. Monterey said.

Erin took two pills as soon as she walked out of the office. She didn't usually take the drug before going to work—she liked to be at her sharpest—but she was still so keyed up from her horrible night that she needed to take the edge off.

By the time the car arrived to take her to work, she'd stopped feeding the prickling need to check her surroundings every five seconds. The elderly gentleman walking his equally elderly dog across the street didn't seem to be a danger to her anymore. That's how ridiculous her anxiety was. Everyone was a potential threat to her safety. The Xanax just helped her act halfway sane.

Dr. Monterey's words crossed her mind as she settled into the backseat of the car, but she pushed them away as quickly as they came. It wasn't the first time the psychiatrist had said something like that to her, but Erin always came to the same conclusion: she had no intention of reliving the trauma of her kidnapping. It was why she hadn't been back to Huntsville in twelve years.

And she had no intention of ever returning.

4

At her desk later that morning, Erin squinted at her computer. The Xanax had taken the edge off the usual anxiety bullshit she had to deal with, but her sleepless night was really catching up to her. Even with her blackout drapes drawn and the office darker than a hungover vampire's lair, her head pounded, and her stomach churned the acid from her coffee.

So here she was, burying every nasty memory that kept her up last night and squinting painfully at her computer screen. She'd once come to work with walking pneumonia, so a headache and nausea weren't going to keep her from doing her job. Her eyes flicked to her locked door. That didn't mean she had to socialize though.

Opening up her email, she groaned when she got

to the "Return Calls" folder, which already had a queue of twenty. These were the clients who weren't content with an emailed response, and much like Christopher Roland, required a phone call to placate them. Nikki helpfully screened her email and added these tedious clients to a folder for her every day.

She picked up her phone receiver with a sigh, but before she could dial, Nikki's distinctive knock rang out.

"Come in," Erin said, replacing the receiver with a click.

"Yeah, I would," Nikki said, sardonic tone traveling through the thick door, "only you have it locked, remember?"

"This better be important," Erin grumbled as she stood painfully.

Nikki held a white bag aloft as Erin opened the door. "I come bearing carbs. Whole grain, of course."

"Of course," Erin said with an eye roll followed by a reluctant smile. "Fine, you're forgiven for making me get up."

"The muffins aren't the only reason I'm here though," Nikki said. "There's a really pushy guy on the phone who says he has to speak to you, and since you've been ignoring my calls and texts since you arrived, I was forced to hunt you down." She gave her an all-suffering look.

"Oh Lord," Erin said around a mouthful of muffin,

the Southern accent she usually kept hidden slipping out just a bit. "Who is it now? I told you after the last time we dealt with a pushy client to just be firm and say they had to make an appointment first."

Last time had been Christopher Roland collapsing in the lobby in hysterics over his latest fashion line being delayed by a week. It had taken Erin nearly three hours to settle him and get him back home.

"Well, I couldn't turn him away—it's a cop."

"Damn. What has Christopher done now?"

Nikki snorted. "This has nothing to do with him for once. It's not even NYPD."

Erin put down the remains of her muffin. "Then where's the cop from?"

Nikki shrugged. "Some county called Broward I think?" Erin froze at the mention of that county— Nikki was butchering the pronunciation of it, so maybe it wasn't what she thought it was, but her heart still raced. "Maybe it's a Chicago suburb or something because that's what his accent sounds like to me—you know, hot but super nasally," she added with a teasing laugh.

Ordinarily Erin would laugh along with her, but she could barely force herself to crack a smile.

"You okay?" Nikki asked with knitted brows. "Your face just went super pale."

"I'm fine—just tired. I don't know if I'm up to dealing with a random cop today," she said as she returned to her desk and sat down heavily. "Can you tell him I'm in meetings all day?"

"Already tried that. He said it was urgent and he'd wait on hold all day and call back the next day if he had to. I don't think he'll be easy to get rid of."

It probably has nothing to do with my past, Erin told herself, even as her palms began to sweat so much she could feel damp marks on her desk.

"Erin," Nikki said with her gaze like a laser, and Erin tensed all over at her serious tone. "You look like you're going to puke all over your desk. If you would just take melatonin and that bedtime tea blend every night and actually eat like a normal human being, I guarantee you wouldn't have all these sleep problems."

"I'll start tonight."

"Uh huh. That's what you always say. Anyway, take the call on line two. I'll step out. Maybe I'll go get you a charcoal smoothie to detox."

"You get me that, and I really will puke on my desk," Erin said with a shudder.

Nikki laughed as she closed the door behind her, and then Erin stared at the blinking red light. A cop calling was never good, and one from her home state was even worse. But her past was behind her. She wasn't that girl anymore.

She took a deep breath, straightened her spine, and picked up the phone.

"This is Erin Masters," she said in her most professional voice.

A pause, and then a deep voice said, "Is this the Erin Masters who used to be known as Erin Lewis?"

Instantly, Erin's mind returned to high school roll call, to her homeroom teacher with her thick country accent calling out "Erin Loo-wis."

From there, all she had to do was think about home, and her stomach churned.

"I haven't gone by that name in a long time." She'd changed it the moment she left West Virginia behind.

"I understand, ma'am," he said in a way that sounded a little awkward with his Midwestern accent. "My name is Detective Adam Herrera, and I sure am relieved to have gotten in touch with you. This is a big case, and there are a lot of similarities even though they're years apart. In fact, it's becoming more and more clear that your cases are linked."

It was clear from the detective's rushed tone that he expected a certain reaction from Erin, but all she could muster was confusion. "I'm sorry...what cases?"

Detective Herrera took a breath. "Did you listen to my voicemails? I didn't want to have to leave them on your phone, but I was desperate to get in touch with you."

Erin thought of the initial missed call from a West Virginia area code that she'd ignored and then blocked.

"No. I don't know what you're talking about. What cases?"

"Thirteen years ago you were the victim of an unsolved kidnapping—"

"Obviously I know about that," Erin snapped before her mind could take her back. She couldn't afford another sleepless night. "What's the other case? What does it have to do with me?"

"Miss Masters, I'm sorry to have to tell you this, but your sister Brooke went missing three days ago."

There was a pause while Erin's sluggish brain processed the information, and then she barely had time to grab the trash can under her desk before vomit splashed all down the sides.

5

E rin wiped her mouth with a tissue, her hand shaking. Images of Brooke's smiling face from her Instagram flashed across Erin's mind. *Missing.* How could that be possible?

"You okay?" the detective asked.

Erin ignored his sympathy. "What happened to Brooke?"

"Your mother, Janet, first reported Brooke missing when she didn't come home from school on Monday," Detective Herrera said, and Erin flinched at the mention of her mother's name. She shouldn't be surprised Janet didn't call and tell her Brooke was missing, considering Janet didn't have Erin's number. She hadn't spoken to her mother since the day she left. *You'll come crawling back, sugar!* Janet had slurred. *They always do.*

"We questioned her friends from school, the teachers, and anyone who might have seen Brooke leave. No one could tell us anything. Her locker held nothing out of the ordinary." Erin kept the tissue pressed against her lips as each thing he said made her feel more and more nauseous. "The only noteworthy thing is that her boyfriend, Steve, is also missing."

Slowly, Erin lowered the tissue. She knew that name—she'd seen it often enough on Brooke's Instagram. A flash of the boy's sandy blonde hair, slightly crooked nose, and wide smile came to her mind. "Wait—Steve is missing, too?"

"Yes, he went missing the same day."

Erin's shoulders sagged forward. "Then they're obviously together. They probably just ran off to party or something. Or, who the hell knows—it's West Virginia. They may have run off to get married."

"Does your sister often skip school and disappear without telling anyone where she is?" Detective Herrera asked, skepticism clear in his tone.

Erin bristled at his question. A real sister would know the answer to that, but all Erin had to go on was what she'd learned about Brooke from Instagram. "I know she parties a lot. And she's young. We all make stupid decisions when we're teenagers. Missing doesn't necessarily mean she was kidnapped." Erin had made a stupid decision once, and it had nearly cost her her life.

"That's true, but there are some aspects of this case that just don't add up. For one, your mama said it's not like Brooke to not come home or tell her where she was going."

Erin snorted. "I find that hard to believe. Janet never cared where anyone was except her dealer." Granted it had been years since Erin had spoken to Janet—the only communication they had now was through an estate attorney who helped establish a college fund for Brooke. Still, Erin couldn't believe her poor excuse for a mother could have changed that much.

"Your sister seems well cared for, though I understand you had a different upbringing," he added, his voice not quite as gruff. Erin didn't respond. "I dug through the other missing person reports for the town —all three of them over the past thirty years or so—as well as other similar investigations. You know how it works in Huntsville. Everyone knows everyone, and they all keep tabs on each other. If Brooke and Steve had run off to get hitched or something, some old busybody would be gossiping about it."

"That doesn't mean this wasn't some kind of spur of the moment idea they both had," Erin said stubbornly. She was desperate for any explanation that didn't involve Brooke being abducted.

"Miss Masters, what happened to you thirteen years ago was one of the cases I pulled. I can't ignore the fact that now a girl who is not only the same age you were when you were taken, but is also your sister, is now missing. And the two of you aren't the only ones. Huntsville hasn't had many missing person cases, but this part of West Virginia is close to Ohio and Kentucky. When I expanded my search to include a thirty-mile radius in other states, I found other girls around the same age and physical description had gone missing. In fact, it's been one girl every year since you disappeared. Unfortunately, none of these girls have been seen again. No one except you, Miss Masters."

Her mouth, already sour-tasting from throwing up, went dry. Her sleek, modern office faded away. In its stead was a dark basement that reeked of mildew and rusting metal. Footsteps rang out on the stairs, and she whimpered.

Hey there, buttercup.

"Are you still there?" the detective asked.

Erin swallowed hard. "Yes."

"Look, I know this is hard. I wouldn't have contacted you if I didn't think you could help. The fact of the matter is, this has been going on under our noses for years, but no one put it together about the other missing girls because they're from outside our jurisdiction. It wasn't until I saw all the cases were within a thirty-mile radius from Huntsville that I thought they could all be related."

"And did those girls go missing with their boyfriends like Brooke?"

"No, the others disappeared like you did—alone."

Every mention of her past made Erin want to end the call, and for a moment, her finger hovered over the disconnect button. He'd just call back though. His voice had that note of interest that bordered on insistence that she'd heard so many times from her clients. "Then it sounds like Brooke's situation is different from all the others. She's probably run away with her boyfriend, which I totally understand given who she lives with. If you knew Janet, you'd want to run away from her, too. I'm sure she'll turn up in a day or two— or even earlier on her social media. From what I can tell, she documents just about every aspect of her life online."

"Using that same logic, then wouldn't she have posted by now? You think she's off partying or even secretly marrying her boyfriend? How can she possibly resist putting something like that up on social media?"

"Well, she's not stupid. She knows that's a good way to get caught. Look, Detective, I appreciate you telling me this and dredging up my past, but I'm going to have to go. I have clients waiting for my call."

"I understand you're busy, and I know you'd rather not talk about your own case, but you have to know it's similar to Brooke's. You disappeared after work one evening when you'd always come straight home to take care of your baby sister. Brooke always goes straight home after school on the days she doesn't have cheerleading because she's in advanced classes and has hours of homework.

"Thirteen years ago, you told the police you escaped in the woods from a house not five miles from the town."

"Yeah, and they never found it," Erin said, gripping the receiver tightly. They never even looked. "I lost all credibility after that."

"Still, that house and even the surrounding area could be an important clue to what's happening now. If you agree to come back to Huntsville, you could be invaluable to the case. We could try and retrace your steps."

Erin felt the muffin she ate earlier rise in her throat, but she managed not to vomit again. "No. *Hell* no. I promised myself I'd never set foot in that shithole of a town again, and I keep my promises to myself. I'm the only one who does."

"Miss Masters—"

"I'm sorry, Detective, but I really have to go."

"Your sister is in danger, Miss Masters…what if you're the only one who can help her?"

"I'm never going back to Huntsville," she said, and then hung up amid his rushed protests.

After a moment's thought, she picked up the phone again and called Nikki. "Hey, if that cop calls again, tell him I'm in meetings all day. I've already wasted too much time this morning as it is."

"You got it, boss lady," she said.

Detective Herrera was wrong. Brooke wasn't kidnapped like her—what would be the chances of that? It seemed impossible. No, the cop had stirred up Erin's past for no damn reason, and her fear was rapidly replaced with a burning need to get some work done. What happened to her was thirteen years ago now. To think that her kidnapping might be related to Brooke's disappearance seemed farfetched and border-line ridiculous. Obviously Detective Herrera was just grasping at anything to help him solve the case. Too bad he was ignoring the most likely scenario: that she'd simply run off. Honestly, in that town, who wouldn't?

Erin pushed all thoughts aside and did what she did best: got on with her fucking life.

By the time Erin got home that night, it was close to nine o'clock. She had to pretend to leave the office when Nikki did and then snuck back in as soon as they were both out of the building just to avoid hearing Nikki's lecture. Work was the only thing that could really distract her, which was why Detective Herrera's phone call in her sanctuary had been like getting home and finding your foolproof safe robbed.

She'd spent hours at work responding to emails, making phone calls, and brainstorming her clients' billboard and ad campaigns. Usually, her whole day flew by happily when she was busy with this part of her job. It was a chance to be creative and artistic, to use her skills to manipulate customers into buying beautiful things they didn't know they needed. Even this hadn't been enough to keep her thoughts at bay. Her conversation with the detective today had ripped open the mental box where she kept her childhood memories locked away.

And now, as she stared around at her apartment, with its gleaming appliances and quartz countertops, she thought of the dingy, cramped house she and Brooke had grown up in. As much as she'd tried to erase the mental images of it, she could still see it just like looking at a picture: cheap, stained linoleum, filthy carpets with cigarette burns, and appliances that only worked every once in a blue moon. She and Brooke had shared one cramped room that only had space for a twin bed. Now she had a king-sized bed just for her.

She sat down heavily on her spotless sofa and tried to unwind by watching Netflix, but she couldn't get past the main menu. With all the thoughts crowding her head, the hundreds of choices proved overwhelming. She let a trailer play over and over while her mind wandered. On the wall adjacent to the flat-screen TV hung her framed diploma from a university in Upstate New York.

It hadn't been the most prestigious school, but it was the only one that had offered her not just admission but a full scholarship. It had made every second of her time spent in the ancient Huntsville library writing essay after essay worth it. After everything she'd been through, she'd never gone back to high school. She got her GED, applied to every college and university on the eastern seaboard, and took the first bus out of town the day after she got the acceptance letter. She would have applied to schools all the way across the country, only she knew she'd never be able to afford to get there. On the bus, she'd chosen a seat in the very back so she could see everyone in front of her, her hands shaking even as she steeled her spine with determination.

In college, she'd avoided any attempts to draw her into a social life. For one thing, she knew she would only excel with a laser focus on her studies. Frat parties weren't her scene; they reminded her too much of life with Janet. In fact, she avoided all parties. She'd watched her mother throw her life away on sex, drugs, and alcohol, and she sure as hell wasn't going to repeat her mistakes.

That didn't mean guys had left her alone. They'd approach her after class or outside her dorm, clearly nervous as they cleared their throats repeatedly or fidgeted, but all she could think of was the moment she was taken. The fear would come over her so strongly she would only manage a stuttered refusal and whirl away back to the safety of her room. There, she'd be eaten alive by guilt, remembering their stricken faces. It wasn't their fault she pictured them suddenly whipping out a rag covered with chloroform and dragging her off to a house in the woods.

It sickened her to still be so affected by what happened to her, so her sophomore year in college she'd tried something different. She didn't wait for some nervous boy to approach her; she asked them out first and slept with them on the first date. Some would call afterward, others wouldn't, and maybe she'd go on another date or two, but that was the end of it. She wasn't going to let some boys get in the way of her academic goals. She made sex about taking control—it was her decision to do it, and always hers to stop. In the back of her mind, though, hung the fear of getting pregnant. Though she'd taken the pill as soon as she could get it from the university health center, and she made every guy she slept with wear a condom, she still feared accidental pregnancy. It was how her mother ended up with her. She'd been sleeping with so many men at the time that she didn't even know which of them was Erin's father, so she'd never even had the benefit of child support.

Whenever Erin thought about her life ending up

like her mother's, it was like standing in front of a yawning grave. She'd rather throw herself in and be buried than wind up an unemployed, alcoholic prostitute with two kids to take care of. Because of this fear, having sex always led to paralyzing thoughts of pregnancy. She would agonize over every little symptom of her body, wondering if it was an early sign of life growing within her, despite knowing it was nearly impossible with two forms of birth control. Still, the anxieties grew, until eventually she went back to avoiding it altogether.

College made shallow relationships easy. One-night stands were the norm, and that suited Erin just fine. It wasn't until she started moving in adult circles that it became a problem. Men would call, expecting to see her again, and on the off chance she agreed to another date, she'd act so cold and off-putting that they'd get the hint.

Relationships had never been a priority. She'd focused on nothing but her schoolwork, and it had paid off. She'd landed a highly competitive internship at a well-known PR firm in the city. From there, she used her single-minded ambitions to climb her way to the top until she'd amassed so many of her own dedicated clients that she left to start her own firm.

Hearing from that detective took her straight back to Huntsville like she'd never left. Like she'd never made something of herself. And Brooke...

She sat down on her couch. *Brooke's fine*, she told herself, and it was a familiar refrain. When she was younger and idealistic, she'd believed she'd become successful and then bring her sister back to live with her. Before she knew it, though, the years raced by, and the more Erin thought about having a teenager to be responsible for, the more she thought that really Brooke would hate living in New York anyway. From all the pictures she'd seen of her sister, she was happy and thriving—despite all odds. She wasn't a little girl anymore, and she didn't need Erin like she had before.

A memory of sleeping curled protectively around her baby sister drifted into her mind, and a tear slipped down Erin's cheek.

She swiped at it and stood. *Brooke's fine*, she told herself again, but that ugly roiling doubt continued to assault her stomach. Blood pounded in her ears, and her jaw ached from keeping it clenched. There was only one thing that could help when she got like this, so Erin strode into her pristine white bathroom and pulled open the medicine cabinet. She shook out a handful of Xanax and swallowed them with a bottle of water.

Erin didn't let herself succumb to the oblivious state that Xanax gave her often, but she wasn't going to let that asshole cop cause her another night's missed sleep.

Thoughts of Brooke slipped into her mind before

the drug could take effect. Even though Erin had seen her sister's pictures online countless times, she still thought of her as four years old. She remembered her high-pitched Minnie Mouse voice when she was chattering away happily to Erin at night. The rest of the time she stayed quiet, just observing with her big eyes. When Erin would take her to the playground after school, Brooke would stand with her little hand in Erin's, just watching the other kids. Erin had learned not to push, that Brooke would go play when she was ready.

Now, as an adult, Erin wondered if her little sister had been trying to determine if the situation was safe or not. It made her heart twist in her chest. She'd grown up with not only a neglectful mother, but in a house that frequently had abusive men shouting and even breaking things. Sometimes they hit Janet, too.

An image flitted through Erin's mind, then: Brooke cowering as a little girl in front of a faceless man with a belt. It never happened when Erin was there—she'd done her best to protect her sister always, but then she'd left. Suddenly, the image shifted, and Brooke was seventeen. The man became the man in the mask who'd taken Erin thirteen years ago.

Erin shuddered and shook her head. No, that was impossible.

I'm so sorry, Brooke, Erin thought, as her mind began to muddle with the effects of the Xanax. Her cheeks were wet as she changed into a nightshirt. She needed the drug to work now, dammit. She couldn't stand the guilt of knowing she'd left her little sister behind.

Within minutes, the medicine slowed Erin's racing heart and caused her eyelids to droop.

Her last thought before it finally worked its magic was: *where is Brooke now?*

E rin woke with a start, scrambling to her feet from a scratchy wool blanket on the floor. A single lightbulb covered the dank basement in a faint, eerie glow. She couldn't see very far beyond where she sat, but her raw nerves sensed his presence.

He loomed above her, a monstrous figure that seemed to be made entirely of shadow. Her heart pounded painfully in her chest as she pushed herself against the cold, unyielding basement wall.

He stepped into the light, holding a tray of food. His head scraped the lowest pipes of the basement ceiling; he seemed impossibly tall, like a giant from some terrible fairy tale. "I brought you supper, kitten." His voice was garbled through the thick ski mask. He offered a tray of steaming mashed potatoes and meatloaf, and Erin's stomach recoiled. She shifted to the right, scanning her surroundings for an escape. There was none "You don't like meatloaf?"

The meatloaf suddenly filled with maggots until the wriggling, white larvae were overflowing the tray and falling to the floor. A scream caught in her throat, and she fought to get away. He only pushed the tray closer, until she could feel the crawling bodies of maggots. Her hand shot out and knocked the whole thing out of his hands, and then he was on her.

All she could smell was stale cigarettes and sour sweat as he pressed himself against her. He grabbed hold of both her arms. She couldn't move. She clenched her jaw closed so tightly it hurt, but still a little whimper escaped.

"Don't be afraid, kitten," he said as he put his nose right up to her hair and inhaled deeply. He wrapped an arm around her trembling middle. "We're going to have some fun."

Suddenly, the nightmare shifted, and Erin became an unwilling observer to this sick performance. Brooke took her place, her features twisted in a mask of fear as the faceless man pushed himself against her. But it wasn't the Brooke she knew now; the girl before her was only four years old. The monstrous, shadowy man held her tight, while Brooke struggled frantically.

"Brooke!" Erin shouted in the dream. She tried to move toward her sister, but she was paralyzed.

Brooke turned toward her. "Help me, Erin," she cried in her little-girl voice, and then the man shoved her down to the floor. Brooke struggled, but she was far too small and weak to fend him off. She reached for Erin desperately, but Erin still couldn't move an inch.

As she watched, the kidnapper became less like a man and more like some demon of the night. Shadowy tendrils flowed off his dark clothes, covering Brooke until she disappeared in the blackness, swallowed whole.

Her scream echoed through the basement, agonizing in its intensity.

E rin awoke with a loud gasp that felt like it sucked all the air out of the room. It took her a moment to get her bearings, to realize she was safe in her own bedroom. Her heart pounded so hard her chest shook with it.

Shadows from the nightlight she still couldn't sleep without made eerie patterns on the floor. She glanced at the clock on her nightstand. It was only half past midnight. She hadn't been asleep long, but it felt like she'd been trapped in that nightmare for hours. Her sheets were twisted around her legs, giving evidence to the thrashing she'd been doing while asleep.

The Xanax had done its job and knocked her out, but it couldn't stop the dreams.

"Fucking cop," she muttered, pushing her sweaty hair off her face. She hadn't had a nightmare in months. She tried not to let the memory of it push its way into her conscious thoughts, but she couldn't stop it.

The nightmare trickled back into her mind in bits and pieces, and she shuddered at the thought of the maggots, of the shadow-man devouring her sister. Seeing Brooke as a vulnerable little girl like that tore Erin apart. Tears filled her eyes, and her whole body shook.

The man was a monster in her dream, but she knew the truth of what he did was so much worse.

Your sister is in danger, Miss Masters…what if you're the only one who can help her?

He was wrong. Brooke had probably already surfaced, and all this panic was for nothing. Disentangling herself from her sheets, Erin grabbed hold of her phone. Quickly pulling up Brooke's profile, she scanned the most recent pictures. Her heart plummeted. The same shot of her smiling with her arms around her boyfriend was still at the top. There was nothing new for four days now.

Despite Erin's efforts to comfort herself, dread filled her stomach like poison. Where was Brooke? Why hadn't she posted?

Erin studied Brooke's smiling face and thought of her own life. Erin had always promised herself she'd take care of her baby sister, and so far, she had failed miserably. Sure she made certain she had plenty of money, but she'd still left Brooke in the care of their worthless, alcoholic mother. Despite that, Brooke had thrived like a stubborn dandelion in asphalt. But what if she'd been taken? What if she was suffering the same fate as Erin?

Images from the terrible nightmare filled her mind: Brooke shifting from a seventeen-year-old to the little girl Erin still thought of her as, crying out for Erin to save her.

In her mind, it echoed every fear she'd ever had for Brooke: that Janet's neglect would end up getting her killed or worse.

But then, what use could Erin be if she did what Detective Herrera asked? How could returning to that shitty town do Brooke any good, even if he was right and she'd been kidnapped? That was a job for the cops, not the owner of a PR firm. Though instead of absolving her of further worry, the thought made her more uncomfortable. She rubbed her arms and stared down at her phone like it might have the answers.

The Huntsville police weren't exactly the NYPD. She didn't know much about Detective Herrera, but if the rest of his department was anything like they were when Erin was a teenager, then Brooke had about as much hope of rescue as a snowstorm in Miami.

The nightmare flitted through her mind again, only this time, the kidnapper wasn't some shadowy demon. He was a man, and that was bad enough. Immediately,

Erin's brain tried to refute the possibility. How could the same kidnapper take Brooke thirteen years later? But it was that niggling doubt that ate at Erin, getting past even the soothing effects of the Xanax.

If there was even a remote chance the horrifying trauma Erin had endured was happening to Brooke right now, then she owed it to her to do everything she could to help. Erin couldn't let Brooke end up like her: broken and alone.

Before she could delve deeper into her fears, Erin pulled up blocked voicemails. All the calls from Detective Herrera were at the top of the messages. She found his number and pressed send with a shaky finger.

Two rings, and then a gruff, sleep-distorted voice answered. "Detective Herrera."

"I'll do it. I'll do whatever it takes to help you find Brooke."

6

THEN

E rin balanced a tray with a greasy burger, fries, and a sweet tea refill as she made her way from the blazing hot short-order cook station to one of the back booths. Her feet ached from the combination of too-tight shoes and being on them for so long. The air was thick with the smell of cigarettes, fat popping on the grill, and cheap plastic furniture. Moving carefully in the tight diner, she had to stifle a yawn as she deposited the plates in front of a rotund trucker with hairy arms and a stained shirt.

"Thanks, honey," he said, with a smile that, while

missing some teeth, at least didn't include a lascivious glance at her body.

"Just let me know if you need anything else," she said with a tired smile.

As she returned with her tray to get the next order, she checked in on Brooke. She looked like a sleeping puppy all curled up in one of the empty booths. A ratty blanket hung off the edge of the bench. Now dingy and beige instead of pink, the blanket had been with Brooke since she was a baby. Erin felt a burst of love just looking at her sister's little hand clutching it so tightly. Beside her was the baby doll Erin had saved up to get her this year. She carried it and the blanket everywhere she went.

Only ten more minutes until midnight, and then Erin and Brooke could finally go home. It was late to keep her baby sister out—late even for Erin, really, on a school night—but she didn't dare leave her alone with their mama. Sleep deprivation in a four-year-old had to be better than the fucked-up mess she'd witness alone with Janet.

At least at Eddie's Diner, they got free dinner and all the leftover day-old pie they could eat. Erin took all the shifts she could get, and that meant working as soon as she finished up school until midnight some nights. Money was so tight it was practically nonexistent, and they had bills to pay. Food stamps only went so far. Besides, Erin was saving up to get her and Brooke the hell out of this town first chance she got.

She grabbed the coffee pot and went to refill the other customer's cup. He thanked her gruffly, hat pulled down low, face badly in need of a shave. She didn't have to look outside at his tractor trailer to know he was another trucker come to refresh himself before moving on again. They were just about the only customers they had—them and random travelers who stopped in off the highway on their way to somewhere better. That's all Huntsville was—just a brief stop. Sometimes she pictured herself begging a ride for her and Brooke off one of these truckers, maybe one of the ones that didn't look at her like she worked at Hooters. She could never bring herself to do it, though. She knew what trying to rely on others got you: jack shit.

By the time she put the coffee pot up and refilled a couple of drinks, the first trucker had wolfed down his burger and fries. Erin stuffed her two-dollar tip in her pocket and carried his plates away.

"You about finished, Erin?" Eddie, the owner of the diner, asked when she deposited the dirty plates in the kitchen.

He was a middle-aged man with a receding hairline and a rather large belly that was always covered by a grease-stained shirt. He worked hard at his diner, often staying as late as the staff. He was nice enough, and he gave her all the hours she wanted to work, but she often caught him looking at her like a piece of meat. He would stand at the grill, flipping burgers but watching her, tongue darting out to lick his greasy lips. It made her skin crawl.

"Yes, sir," she said. "I was fixing to head home with Brooke in just a minute." She nodded toward the booth where Brooke slept with a regretful look. She'd rather let her sleep as long as she wanted, but it was a long way home, and she didn't think she could carry her.

"You gonna walk home?" When Erin nodded, he picked up his keys. "I'm on my way out, so why don't I just give you two a ride?"

Erin debated it for a moment. Eddie had given her some lascivious looks before, but so far, he'd never acted on them. And she badly needed a ride. She glanced out the filmy window to see that it had started to rain—just drizzling now, but it threatened to pour. It made the night sky even darker, no moon or stars in sight. "I'd appreciate that."

"Get your things and I'll meet you out front."

After putting up her apron and collecting the last of her tips, Erin carefully scooped up Brooke and her toys. Brooke didn't even stir; she just hung limply in her arms. Erin smiled down at her, her heart swelling in her chest. Her baby sister was so innocent and trusting; she could fall asleep anywhere. Erin wished she could sleep that deep, but she hadn't in years.

Outside, Eddie waited by his big, four-door pickup truck. He held open the back door, and Erin carefully laid Brooke down on the seat. She tried to buckle her as best she could, but she figured there wouldn't be many cars out on the road anyway. Better to let her sleep than to wake her up just to fasten the seatbelt properly.

"You just come on up here with me," Eddie said when he saw Erin meant to squeeze in next to her sister. "Ain't hardly any room back there."

He had a point as the majority of his back seat was taken up by banking boxes, miscellaneous clothing, and other odds and ends.

After a brief hesitation, Erin climbed up into the passenger seat of the pickup. Eddie turned on the radio to a country station and kept the volume low. With the rumble of the engine and the dark night outside, Erin struggled to stay awake. She didn't realize the bone-deep exhaustion affecting her body until she'd stopped moving. As they drove through their two- stoplight town, Erin's eyes drifted closed.

When she woke again, a country singer was still crooning with a twangy guitar in the background, but the truck had stopped moving. She turned her head to look at Eddie and realized with a start that he'd moved across the dividing armrest and was now only inches away. He ran his hand up her bare thigh, a lecherous grin on his face.

Erin immediately recoiled. "What the hell are you doing?"

"I thought you'd wanna thank me for bringing you home. The whole town knows this is how your mama thanks everyone—figured you wouldn't be much different."

Erin's stomach clenched and her ears buzzed. Before she could even stop to consider it, she slapped him in the face hard enough to make her hand sting.

"Don't you ever compare me to my mama," she said and shoved the door open.

"Little bitch," he said as she gathered Brooke up. "You can walk home next time!"

The pickup peeled away from the curb, nearly knocking Erin off-balance, and her arms shook from the adrenaline of fighting back. She closed her eyes for a moment, tears building behind them.

That's when she saw the car parked out front. It was a shiny new sedan and looked as out of place in front of their house as a mongrel at a fancy dog show. That could only mean one thing.

She shifted Brooke higher in her arms and stalked toward the collapsing front porch. She had to avoid the second step as it was partially rotted out and would give way under their combined weight. Even with the dim porch light, anyone could tell the house was a hovel, with peeling paint that used to be white but was now gray. The screen door that served as their front door wasn't even closed completely. Erin's lip curled as she stepped inside with Brooke.

Cigarette smoke and musty, stagnant air enveloped them, making Brooke cough. That was partly from the house being so filthy. Brooke's toys were everywhere, and there were dirty plates and cups covering the old coffee table. Rotting food mixed with beer wafted from the overflowing garbage can in the empty kitchen as Erin passed by.

The moment Erin saw her mama's bedroom door ajar with tell-tale noises coming from within, she pulled Brooke closer to herself. They'd have to pass by to get to their shared room, and the last thing she wanted was for Brooke to get an eyeful of whatever their mama was up to in there.

A low voice came from Janet's bedroom, and Erin's stomach dropped. She tried to walk quickly past, but she still caught sight of the scene inside. Her mama guzzled the contents of a half-empty whiskey bottle. A sheet covered her lower half as she lounged across her bed with breasts exposed. A tall man with sandy blonde hair stood over her buckling his belt. He dropped a few bucks on her mama's nightstand, and as he turned, he made eye contact with Erin.

It was Pastor Dave from the church downtown. He winked at Erin, and she hurried to her own room with Brooke. She locked the flimsy door behind her and laid her baby sister down on the bed. Waves of disgust rolled over Erin as she waited to hear the sedan leave. When it finally did a few minutes later, she collapsed into bed and curled herself around Brooke.

Only then did she let the tears come, hot and furious as she shook the bed with her quiet sobs. This was why Erin got treated like a whore when she was only seventeen. Her mama let men pay her for sex, and everyone knew it. Was it any wonder they thought maybe Erin would too?

She made a promise to herself that night: she'd do whatever she had to do to get out of this snakepit of a town.

7

NOW

With her small suitcase trailing behind her, Erin walked through Yeager Airport, her head pounding with a splitting headache. She wasn't even in Huntsville yet, but her muscles had been tense since she left New York. The worst part of the flight was that West Virginia was so damn beautiful. It was mountainous and lush this time of year, and the vistas were breathtaking enough that she almost forgot where she was going.

When she stepped outside the airport, a line of cars waited to pick people up, and she had to search for a few moments before she found the older SUV Detective Herrera said he'd be driving. The man behind the wheel was dark-haired and wearing aviators. When he got out, she noticed that he wasn't in uniform. Instead he wore jeans and a tight shirt that showed off his muscles and copious arm tattoos. He was nothing like she expected, and for a moment, she just stood there stupidly.

"Erin, right?" he asked with a smile. It was a nice smile; sort of crooked, but with straight, white teeth. "Can I help you with that?"

When she nodded, he grabbed hold of her suitcase and put it in the back of the SUV.

"Thank you."

He held open the passenger door for her, but she didn't immediately move toward it.

Last night, when he'd offered to pick her up from the airport, she'd readily agreed. She figured it would be the quickest way to get to Huntsville and find out for herself what had happened to Brooke. But now that she was faced with the prospect of getting in a stranger's car, her mouth went dry. Of course, when she'd agreed to it, she'd imagined him wearing his cop uniform. This man could be anyone.

"This probably isn't as nice as you're used to," he said with an almost nervous swipe of his hand through his thick hair, "but it's clean—well, cleaner than it was anyway."

Erin struggled to channel that strong, confident

executive who owned her own firm. "This is fine, but I was expecting to see you in uniform."

Detective Herrera must have picked up on her suspicious tone because he pulled out a badge from his back pocket. "I'm just off duty today. That's why I'm in plain clothes and driving around my old gas guzzler."

Erin's shoulders relaxed. "Thanks for proving your identity," she said and flashed a small smile his way. She wouldn't apologize for being suspicious though. After everything she'd been through, she'd be an idiot to just hop into a stranger's car with no questions asked.

"No problem."

A security officer at the airport waved at them to move on, so Erin finally got into the SUV. Detective Herrera jogged around to other side and got behind the wheel.

As he pulled away from the curb, he glanced at her. "I know this is hard for you, so I can't tell you enough how thankful I was to get your call that you changed your mind."

"I owe it to Brooke to help in any way I can. Where should we start?"

"That's up to you. Did you want to check into your hotel first, settle in, or did you want to get right into it?"

"I'm here to look for Brooke, not relax in a flea-bitten Huntsville hotel. So, I definitely choose the second option."

He nodded. "I like it. We'll talk with your mother first—see if anything she says about Brooke's disappearance triggers memories for you."

Erin shifted uncomfortably in her seat. "I wasn't expecting having to face Janet so soon, although I know I shouldn't be surprised."

Detective Herrera grew quiet for a moment while he merged onto the highway. "I don't know what your mother was like when you were a kid, but she seems to be very involved in Brooke's life. I've met a lot of mothers who just didn't give a damn, and she isn't one of them. She's desperate to find Brooke."

Erin snorted in disbelief. "Maybe we're talking about two different women."

He gave her a crooked smile, and then they both fell silent as the miles went by. The last time Erin had been on this highway, she'd been on her way out of town. She thought of that scared but determined girl, with five hundred dollars of hard-earned cash in her bag, clothes, and not much else. She never thought she'd be back here.

They drove past thick forests and scenic mountains, but it only made Erin think of her frantic race through the woods. This would never be her happy place. New York City, with its soaring skyscrapers made of glass and metal, clusters of buildings of concrete and brick, and sparse vegetation, had become Erin's sanctuary. She even avoided Central Park because the heavily wooded areas reminded her too much of West Virginia.

All too soon, the detective exited onto the one road through town. On the outskirts, they approached a rundown-looking diner, "Eddie's" scrawled lazily across the top in faded red and white paint. Erin couldn't believe it was still there.

Detective Herrera slowed as they got closer to it. "I should have asked you before—are you hungry?"

"That's nice of you to ask," she said as her stomach rebelled at the thought. "But I wouldn't eat there if I was starving to death. Bad memories," she added when he looked at her with eyebrows raised.

"Fair enough. Somewhere else then?"

Erin thought of her stomach, currently twisting itself in knots. "I'm good."

They fell silent again as they rolled through Main Street, and Erin battled the nostalgia that made her heart sick. There wasn't a building taller than two stories anywhere she looked; the mountains in the distance dwarfed the small town. Compared to the homage to modernism that was most of New York City, with its crowded streets and subway system, Huntsville made you feel like you were going back in time. And not to a particularly nice time—just one where there was a distinctive lack of modern conveniences. Power lines crisscrossed over the roofs of tightly-packed, ancient brick buildings that served as "downtown." Store awnings were tired and faded, and every sign had a weathered look, like it had been hanging there since Lincoln was president.

Instead of ritzy hotels, five-star restaurants, and shops where you could buy anything imaginable, Huntsville's downtown featured a feed and sundries store, hardware shop, and a pharmacy. She could just make out the lone McDonald's beyond Main Street, located on the only intersection with a streetlight.

But when they got to Huntsville High School, Erin pressed herself against the window. It looked nothing like when she went there—less old-fashioned brick schoolhouse and much bigger and more industrial— but she recognized it from some of Brooke's posts.

Seeing the high school in person made her have unpleasant memories of dreading going to school so much that she would get sick. Even now as an adult, her palms began to sweat and she swallowed hard against a sudden queasiness. How could Erin have never come back for Brooke? How could she have made excuse after excuse about her career, her apartment, her *life*, and let this horrible thing happen to someone she loved?

Brooke might still be okay, she reminded herself, but her jaw flexed painfully. She was running on only a few hours of sleep and a disgusting smoothie Nikki had made her choke down before getting on the plane. Her whole body was like a rubber band pulled as far as it would go.

Instead of continuing on past the railroad tracks where her mama's rundown old shack used to be hunched among the weeds, Detective Herrera turned onto a tree-lined street just past the school. The houses here weren't mansions, but they were well-cared for, with huge trees and meticulous landscaping. Just as she was about to ask if possibly Detective Herrera lived in this neighborhood, he stopped in front of a lovely gray Craftsman-style home with white trim. Flowers bloomed on either side of the porch that was complete with rocking chairs.

"Whose house is this?" Erin asked, though she'd already guessed.

"This is your mom's place. I figured we'd start here and let you get the details straight from her."

The house couldn't be further than the dilapidated shack she'd grown up in, and Erin tried unsuccessfully to picture the Janet she'd known with one who could live in this nice of a place. Her mouth went dry, and she reached in her bag for a bottle of water before remembering that she'd drunk her last one on the plane.

She straightened her clothes when she got out of the car and thanked herself for having the foresight to wear her anti-wrinkle pencil skirt and blouse, though she'd been tempted to rough it in joggers and a tank top. The skirt made her look smart and in control even after a cramped plane ride.

Detective Herrera took the lead, and they climbed up the flagstone steps. The front door and trim were spotless, like they were sporting a fresh coat of paint. Two flowerpots overflowing with ivy and some sort of colorful blooms stood on either side of the door. Erin stared at the pretty picture of the porch, momentarily dumbfounded. Since when could Janet keep house?

Before Detective Herrera could ring the doorbell, a man Erin had never met opened the door.

"I thought that was you, detective," the man said, and he was a lot like the picturesque front porch in that he couldn't be further from Janet's typical boyfriend. With his khaki pants and a knit shirt, he looked like he'd just returned from golfing. He appeared to be roughly in his fifties with a receding hairline and a warm smile. He was nothing like the men Janet usually brought home.

"And you must be Erin," he continued as he waved them inside. "It's nice to finally meet you. I'm Phil, your mom's husband."

Erin stared at this man with his sensible clothing and lack of tattoos and heroine tracks. For a moment, she was stunned. When had Janet gotten married? It had never been a priority for her before.

Suddenly a voice called out from upstairs, "Detective Herrera? Is that you?"

Erin knew it had to be Janet, but it sounded nothing like the hoarse, breathy voice she'd always known. They hadn't spoken in ten years at least— everything always went through Erin's lawyer.

Janet raced down the steps and stopped dead when she spotted Erin. Her mother was wearing a bright sundress of all things—Erin wasn't sure she'd ever seen her wear anything nicer than a tank top and denim shorts—with her hair curled flatteringly around her face, Janet barely looked like the mother she'd known. Gone was the bleach-blond hair with dark roots. In its place was a more natural chocolate brown. She even wore fresh makeup that hadn't bled into raccoon eyes. As Janet's gaze drifted over Erin's expensive clothes and upswept hair, her eyes widened when they landed on her face, like it had taken her a moment to recognize her own daughter. Erin tried not to feel insulted; she hardly recognized her mother either.

When she looked to Phil as if for reassurance, it struck Erin how well they fit together—at least from looks alone.

"What is she doing here?" Janet asked, her gaze narrowed at Erin.

"She's here to help with the case," Detective Herrera said, his tone calm.

"She has a name," Erin said, hackles raised at the

combination of her mother's unwelcome stare and Detective Herrera's placating.

"Why didn't you tell me she'd be here?" Janet asked with an annoying emphasis on the "she." Erin immediately knew she'd made a mistake by letting her mother know it bothered her. She'd always been a vindictive bitch.

Phil cleared his throat. "Honey, we thought it might be best if you spoke to each other in person."

Janet whipped her head toward Phil. "You knew? You knew he'd bring her here? Not a single phone call in ten years, and then the second our lives are a mess, she shows up."

Suddenly, Erin was seventeen again, facing off against her wasted, insane mother. "This was a mistake." She turned to go, but Detective Herrera reached out a gentle hand to stop her.

"We're all here to help Brooke," he said. "Including Erin. She flew all the way down from New York to help you find her."

"She doesn't even know Brooke anymore," Janet said with arms crossed. She still wouldn't address Erin directly. "How can she help?"

"As I'm sure you remember, Erin went through something similar when she was Brooke's age. She's not the only one, either. I believe there have been other girls over the years—other disappearances that have gone unsolved. I think they might be connected. Erin could potentially have vital information that helps us track down Brooke."

Phil listened closely, his head nodding and brow furrowed in thought. Janet, on the other hand, snorted in disbelief. "That's how she's supposed to help? By reliving some insane fantasy she made up as a teenager?"

A switch inside Erin flicked. It was thirteen years ago, and she, in her teenage naivety, actually believed Janet would listen to her. But she'd reacted to it like she did everything else in Erin's life: with scorn. "I didn't make it up," Erin said, her fist curled tightly at her side.

When she thought back to that horrible night, it was shocking that there was even a police report of her kidnapping. Her mother had done nothing, as usual.

Janet scoffed again with an added eye roll, and Erin's anger broke free like a wrecking ball.

"I wouldn't expect you to remember that time too well, considering how you were so drunk and high that you hadn't even noticed your oldest daughter—the one who literally did everything around the house, including taking care of her baby sister—went missing for a week."

Janet had the decency to flush, but then her eyes flashed. "How dare you try and make all of this about you when my little girl is missing! You've always been selfish."

"Oh that's rich considering I was the one who took

care of Brooke, went to high school, and worked, while you slept with the entire town and shot up to oblivion. You're a horrible person and an even worse mother."

Janet reared back like she'd been slapped. "You have no right to say that, Erin. You have no idea how hard it was to change, and you weren't here to see it. You couldn't wait to leave us behind, and you never once looked back."

"Of course I know how hard it is to change—I had to do it! I couldn't let you drag me down while you whored around in this white trash town. You should be glad that I got out, but you're not. You've hated every moment of my success. What kind of a mother does that?"

Janet shook with what Erin knew was rage. If it had been thirteen years ago, she would have slapped Erin so hard in the mouth that she would have bled. Now, though, she could only cling impotently to her new fancy husband. "I told you before, Erin. Brooke doesn't need you. We don't need your help either. Just go back home—wherever that is. Get out of here!" she yelled before turning and sobbing into Phil's chest.

Erin watched in disgust as Phil rubbed her mother's back soothingly as she wailed that she didn't deserve any of this. He met Erin's gaze, censure clear in his muddy brown eyes. "I think it's best if you leave."

Before Detective Herrera could stop her, Erin turned on her heel and strode to the door. "Gladly."

8

E rin waited for Detective Herrera inside his car, her heart pounding like she'd just gotten off her exercise bike. How dare Janet call her selfish when she was the most self-centered, horrible mother she could imagine. Wolves raised their offspring better. The way Janet had scoffed at the memory of Erin's kidnapping cut her deep. Deeper than she cared to admit. It brought everything back in a rush:

Finally making it home, tired and bleeding from her flight in the woods, stupidly expecting Janet to welcome her home with open arms, crying in relief.

She got none of that, of course. Janet had simply demanded to have some of the money Erin made—like she had been away the whole time working extra shifts at Eddie's. Erin hadn't even been able to talk to her that night since Janet was so drunk. It was only the next day when Erin had broken down sobbing, reaching for her mother, but Janet had pushed her away. "Don't give me the fake waterworks. I know you were just off with some boy."

And now, despite all the years that had gone by, apparently Janet's opinion hadn't changed.

The driver's door opened, jolting Erin from her reverie. She hastily swiped at the tears on her cheeks.

"You okay?" Detective Herrera asked gently.

"I'm fine. That was just Janet being Janet."

Detective Herrera shook his head. "I'm sorry about that. She's never been so confrontational in all the times I've talked to her. I didn't think you would be at each other's throats. If I did, I would have at least given you a night to rest first."

Erin shrugged. "Better to get it over with right away, I guess."

"Well, I can take you someplace to eat first if you want, or I can just drop you off at your hotel."

Erin smiled. "Don't you mean 'motel'? Calling it something as classy as a hotel is like saying a diner is a fine eatery."

The detective pretended to look affronted. "That's Huntsville's finest inn right there."

"As long as it's halfway clean and has a working shower I'll be okay."

After that meeting with Janet, she still didn't think

she could eat, so she asked him to take her straight to the hotel.

As the SUV quietly rolled through town, Erin turned to Detective Herrera. "How long has Janet been married to Phil anyway?"

"They've been together since I came to town four years ago. I think they've been married a long time. He's just as concerned about Brooke as Janet is."

"Must be nice to have a father who cares," Erin said, thinking of the endless parade of men Janet brought into their house—all of them there for one thing only. Well, two if you included the drugs. At least her mother had pulled it together enough to know who Brooke's father was. She'd even dated him for a year or two—by far her longest relationship. Erin could still remember him, with his gentle smile and thinning hair. Brooke got her sweet nature from him, but even his patience only went so far. He'd left a few months after she came into the world, lacking the fortitude to stand up to Janet and keep her on the wagon. That made Phil the only father-figure Brooke had ever known.

"He's definitely one who cares. You didn't catch their press conference after she turned up missing, I'm guessing?"

Erin turned to him in surprise. "No."

"Sometimes the cameras make even the best parents a nervous wreck, and then they end up looking stilted and detached—or worse, uncaring. But Janet and Phil did great. They both are deeply worried and asked for the public's help finding Brooke."

Erin pulled out her phone and searched for the press meeting in question. She found it right away. She had to skim the video because it was too infuriating to watch. Phil and Janet looked tired and fearful as they spoke into the microphone, cameras flashing. Janet gripped Phil's arm, and he seemed to be fighting back tears.

"Please, just help me find my baby," Janet said at the end, tears glistening prettily in her eyes.

It was a far cry from the dead-eyed look she'd given Erin when she arrived home bruised and battered. Maybe Phil had done more than just clean Janet up. Maybe he'd managed to help her act like a real mother.

"The town responded well, and they organized a search for her and Steve. So far, nothing's turned up. After I pick you up tomorrow, I thought we could head over to the school to talk to her friends and teachers."

"You didn't do that when you first discovered her missing?"

"Two other officers conducted the initial interviews, but that was before I did some research and uncovered the link between your disappearance and hers. I'd like to ask again in light of what happened to you."

Erin searched his face, trying to read between the

lines. "You don't trust that the others did a thorough job in their questioning?"

"Let's just say I'd rather do my own investigating."

"If the cops now are anythinglike they were when I was a teenager, then you should absolutely do follow-up interviews with everyone they've talked to. In fact, since you aren't from around here, it's better if you go full lone wolf and just do everything yourself. Don't leave anything up to them."

He shot her a pointed look. "I'll keep that in mind."

She'd rather endure another awkward meeting with Janet than face going to the school. Erin couldn't even let herself think of those days but coming here made it impossible to avoid. If her baby sister was suffering the same fate…Erin swallowed the lump in her throat. She thought about how her kidnapper toyed with her for the first few days, feeding off her fear sadistically. But then things took a much darker turn.

Detective Herrera slowed to a stop in front of the Huntsville Inn—the only motel in town. Before Erin got out, she turned to the detective. "If he got Brooke —the same guy who had me—then she only has one more day."

"Until what?"

"Until she's broken forever."

Erin sat down on the motel bed, too tired even to strip what was undoubtedly a germ-ridden bedspread. The room had a lingering odor of cigarette smoke that made Erin's skin crawl. The walls held further evidence of years of tobacco exposure with a grimy film tinting the paint a horrible yellowish-beige. Generic artwork featuring boring watercolor landscapes decorated the sparsely-furnished room, and there was only an old ice bucket with cups instead of a mini fridge. The bathroom held a shower and tub combo that she despised because she never felt clean after showering in one. She glanced down at the carpet and grimaced. The navy blue color hid stains, yes, but given the state of the rest of the room, she decided she would be better off never walking on it barefoot. No telling when it had last been cleaned.

As her mind brought forth a review of the horrible day, she grabbed hold of her purse and pulled out the bottle of Xanax. Hell if she was going to try and endure this trip without some pharmaceutical aid. She shook out far more pills than prescribed and gulped them down with a bottle of water.

Curling on her side on the scratchy bleached sheets, she pulled out her phone. Brooke's Instagram page still hadn't been updated, but Erin couldn't stop looking at her smiling face. She looked so much like Erin did at that age: curvy, long legs, long hair. Was that why he'd taken her? Were Brooke and Erin and other teens like them his type?

Where was she?

Erin held the phone tightly like a talisman—praying with everything in her that her sister had just run off with her boyfriend.

"I won't even be mad," she whispered to the picture of Brooke.

And even if she wasn't with her boyfriend, then it didn't necessarily mean that the same guy who'd taken Erin all those years ago took Brooke, too, right? What were the chances of that?

"Ridiculous," Erin mumbled to herself, her eyes growing heavy.

But even as she drifted off, the anxious part of her brain whispered frantic questions, like: what if Detective Herrera's instincts were right?

What if *he* had her?

9

THEN

English was the last class of the day and also the worst. Stephanie and her two lemmings sat behind Erin and basically used the entire period to practice emotional torture. Today was especially bad, though, because Erin had gotten home so late from work last night that she hadn't had time to shower, fix her hair, or even change her clothes. She'd just passed out in bed, dead asleep until her alarm for school went off. And then she'd slept through it. Twice. So now she sat in class with her hair in a ratty bun wearing the same clothes she'd worn yesterday.

"She must really love that hideous t-shirt to wear it

two days in a row," Stephanie said, and her friends snickered. Erin's whole body stiffened.

"Or she's too poor to have more than one," Jenny said.

"It's her hair that really grosses me out," Sara added in a loud whisper.

Erin managed to ignore them until almost the end of class when Stephanie tapped her on the shoulder. Erin didn't turn around, but Stephanie handed her a piece of paper they'd clearly all worked on during class.

How to practice good hygiene:

1. Take a fucking shower because you smell like a whore.
2. Change your clothes every day and if you don't have extra then stop being poor and get some.
3. Wash your nasty hair!!

All three of them laughed so hard it drew the attention of the rest of the class.

"Fuck *off*," Erin yelled, balling up the paper and throwing it at Stephanie.

The girls laughed at Erin's sudden outburst, and all she could think about was putting her hands around Stephanie's slim neck.

When the others went silent, Erin looked up to see

their teacher, Rick, standing over them.

"Erin, I need to see you after class."

The other girls snickered, and Erin shot a glare their way. She could feel the tears building at the back of her throat. The bell rang, signaling the end of what had been a miserable school day.

"Good luck with Mr. Holland, trailer trash," Stephanie whispered as she and the other kids left the classroom.

As soon as Erin was alone with her teacher, she burst into tears. He went and closed the door before returning to her side.

"I hate them all so fucking much," Erin said, her voice thick from crying.

Rick leaned forward and wiped her tears away. "I know it hurts now, but none of them matter. They're all sad, miserable bitches—just like their mothers. Dumb, too. They're all failing my class, you know." Erin looked up at that, and he smiled at her. "It doesn't help their case that they're so mean to my girl." She blushed.

"I read your latest paper, and it was absolutely incredible. You're writing on the college level already, and it's no wonder you have a 4.0."

This made Erin stop crying immediately. "Really? You think I have a chance at scholarships then?"

"Absolutely. I think the universities will fight over you." When a smile broke out across Erin's face, Rick leaned in to kiss her. "You're so beautiful when you smile."

He deepened the kiss, and Erin leaned into him, her heart soaring on his praise. He'd written five glowing recommendations for her to include with her scholarship applications, and it was the most loving thing anyone had ever done for her.

His roving hands went up her shirt to her breasts, and he moved closer until she could feel the hardness of him against her leg.

"I want you so bad," he said as he kissed her neck. "You know how much I love you."

Erin's breaths were coming fast, but she still pushed him back gently. "I love you, too, but I'm not ready. Not until we can be together."

Rick sighed as he ran his fingers down Erin's cheek. "The minute you turn eighteen, I'm leaving my wife. We've been over this." He leaned closer to whisper in her ear. "But that doesn't mean we can't enjoy ourselves until then."

His tongue darted into her ear and she wiggled away, letting out a little laugh. "I just can't do that yet. I'm sorry."

She thought of her mother, of how easily she spread her legs for any man, and Erin had sworn she would live differently. That the first time she had sex would be for love.

A shadow raced across Rick's face, and he gestured

toward his obvious arousal. "You're just going to tease me then? Do you have any idea what this does to me? I'll have to go home and have sex with Norma just so my balls don't burst."

Erin hated when he mentioned Norma, and he'd sworn before they weren't even having sex anymore.

He must have noticed the hurt and dismay in her eyes because he added, "Well, there's a way to avoid all that." He unzipped his pants. "You could help me out right here and now."

Erin hesitated. Was oral sex the same as regular sex? But then she thought of everything Rick had done for her, the recommendation letters, the phone calls where she vented about her nightmare of a mother, and she knew she'd do anything to keep him in her life.

She knelt down in front of him, and even though she'd never done it, she'd walked in on Janet enough times to have a general idea of what to do. Still, she couldn't bring herself to just jump right into it. She didn't want to be like Janet—even for a man she loved.

Unsure how to tell Rick no, she glanced up at him.

"What are you waiting for?" he demanded, a flash of irritation on his face before it settled back into a persuasive smile. "I'm going to explode if you don't touch me now."

Erin took a deep breath. "I'm just not sure—"

But then Rick grabbed her head and forced her down on him.

Before she could wrench herself away, the class-room door swung open. In walked the principal, who took one look at what was going on and came to an immediate stop.

"What the fuck is going on here?" he bellowed.

10

NOW

Detective Herrera came to pick Erin up early in the morning, and all the pills she took the night before made her head spin. Compared to the busy, noisy mornings in New York, with congested roads and throngs of people hurrying to work, the quiet here was unnerving and did nothing to help her feel grounded. Not even the cloudless sky and bird song cheered her. And though the city in fall always rejuvenated her—the crisp air, the chance to wear new boots, the lack of sewer smells after a summer of holding her breath past every grate—the slight chill in the air here only made her glad she'd packed a sweater.

"Coffee?" Adam offered, holding a travel cup aloft as she climbed groggily into his SUV. "I didn't know how you took it, so I just got a bunch of those creamers and sugar packets."

She smiled gratefully at him. "Black is fine." She took a sip and waited for the caffeine to start chasing away some of the fog in her brain. "No doughnuts though?"

He grinned back at her. "Only on special occasions."

Today he was dressed in uniform, the dark blue handsome against his black hair and chestnut skin. He looked nothing like the good old boy cops she was familiar with from her youth. For one thing, he was physically fit. He looked like he worked out pretty hard on a daily basis, with a trim waist and cut arm muscles. It was a far cry from the older, paunchy cops she remembered. The ones who ate too many doughnuts and were slow to answer her call whenever a "boyfriend" of Janet's got too rough.

She stole a look at him, with his styled hair and aviators. "So what's a guy like you doing in a place like Huntsville?"

He glanced her way before turning smoothly onto another road. "It's pretty rare to see a Latino guy this far from a big city, I know."

Erin shook her head. "Okay, I can see how you'd think I meant your ethnicity given where we are. You must get asked fifty times a day about your cultural background given the level of ignorance in this town. No, I meant I can tell by your accent that you're not from Huntsville. I've never known anyone to move here. Most people have been stuck here for generations. The smart ones leave."

"I do get asked that a lot, actually," he said with a laugh. "And you're right. I'm not from around here. I used to be a detective in Chicago."

"Chicago? Wow. Big change coming here. It must be boring as hell in comparison."

Adam kept his eyes on the road and didn't glance her way. "I like the quiet."

He didn't elaborate on his past, so Erin didn't press him. She knew how that was. And anyway, all she could think about was how they were getting closer to the school. It looked different now, sure, but already Erin's mind was churning, thinking of all the horrible memories in that place: Stephanie and all her nasty friends, pedophile Rick, and even the disgusting smell of disinfectant and cafeteria food.

To distract herself, she pulled up her email. Even though she'd neglected her phone for the past twenty-four hours, there weren't many messages that had gone unanswered. That was thanks to Nikki, who, as usual, was completely on top of things.

"You never take a vacation, so you should take all the time you need," she'd said when Erin called her tearfully at three in the morning. "I'll handle everything here."

"It's definitely not a vacation, but thank you so much Nikki. I know I can count on you."

When Adam turned onto the school's street, Erin gritted her teeth and kept her eyes on her phone. The emails blurred as her heart beat faster.

This is ridiculous, she thought. *I'm an adult now.* She shouldn't be afraid of high school.

"The principal agreed to meet with us and let us speak to two of Brooke's best friends," Adam said.

Erin stiffened. "Who's the principal?"

"She hasn't been here long. Her name is Betty Taylor."

Erin let her breath out in a rush. Of course it wasn't the same principal she'd humiliated herself in front of all those years ago.

"I don't know her, thankfully," she said.

Erin reluctantly followed the detective into the school, where they immediately turned right to head into the office. Unlike the dark, cramped hallways she remembered, the high school now featured wide halls with big windows that let in plenty of natural light. She could almost pretend they were somewhere else.

Among the usual school office staples like horrible inspirational posters and an enormous receptionist desk, the space had high ceilings and windows with views of the courtyard.

Erin curled her lip at the poster closest to her that read "Be the Best You Can Be."

An older lady with a poufy hairstyle from three decades ago watched them from behind a tall desk.

"We're here to see Principal Taylor," Adam said.

"Oh! Oh yes of course," she said, before appearing for a moment unsure what to do next. After seeing Adam, she seemed suddenly unable to form a coherent thought. Erin watched with bemusement, wondering if it was due to his looks or to his job title.

Finally, the secretary called Principal Taylor, who turned out to be in the room right beside the office. She probably heard them come in, but Erin thought they wanted to make the whole visit seem more official.

Principal Taylor was tall and slim, with dark hair kept in an un-styled bob. She wore the typical pant suit that women seemed to think made them look more authoritative but always seemed dowdy to Erin.

"I thought you could talk to Brooke's friends in here," she said after introductions had been made. She pointed to a nearby conference room.

"That'll work," Adam said, and Principal Taylor nodded brusquely.

"Melanie, will you call Tiffany Hawthorne and Amanda Wilson's teachers and ask them to meet us here please?"

"Yes, of course," Melanie said in a breathy rush, grabbing up her phone.

"They've been anxious to talk to you," Principal Taylor said while they waited. "Everyone is worried sick over Brooke. She's just the best person—everyone loves her. You know how she is," she added to Erin, since she'd been introduced as Brooke's sister, "always helpful and kind to everyone she meets."

Erin smiled and nodded like she knew. At the same time, it stabbed her heart to know she didn't.

It wasn't long before they were joined by two girls who seemed vaguely familiar to Erin from some of Brooke's Instagram posts. They were both beautiful and athletic-looking, and Erin remembered she'd seen them in cheerleading uniforms with Brooke.

The girl who was introduced as Tiffany had a lovely dark complexion and wore her hair in braids pulled into a ponytail. Her eyes welled up when she saw Adam, and she slumped down in one of the chairs.

Amanda, Brooke's other best friend, reminded Erin of Stephanie, but only in looks. She was tall with delicate features and long, blonde hair. When she sat down and threaded her arm through Tiffany's to offer her strength, Erin knew she was nothing like her old tormentor.

Adam waited until the principal closed the door behind them and returned to her office before talking to them. "Thank you for agreeing to meet with us. I just had some follow-up questions about Brooke that I wanted her sister to hear the answers to."

Their eyes landed hard on Erin. She knew what they were thinking: "Brooke has a sister?"

"Can you tell us how Brooke was acting these past few weeks? Any changes in her behavior?"

They both shook their heads, and Tiffany answered, "No, she's just been acting like Brooke. Too nice for her own good and just annoyingly cheerful." She choked up on the last word. "That's what I always tell her. That she belongs in a Disney movie or something."

Amanda agreed. "The only strange thing that happened was when she didn't show up to cheer the other day. She *always* shows up to practice. I don't think she's missed a single one."

"Remember that time she came with the stomach flu and Miss Cindy had to make her leave?"

Amanda groaned and nodded. "Yes! She kept running off to throw up and then she was back at it."

Erin had to smile to herself at that. It sounded so much like what Nikki said about her the last time she refused to stay home from work. They had more in common than she'd thought. It reminded her of when Brooke was little and she would wrinkle her nose when she laughed, just like Erin. Her smile faded, though, when she thought that Brooke might have something else in common with her big sister. Like being kidnapped.

"It definitely sounds unusual that she didn't go to practice the other day then," Adam said. "Did you talk and text often?"

"Like every minute," Tiffany said. "We have about five different group texts going, but Amanda, Brooke, and I always text each other at least a few times a day."

"And you haven't heard anything from her?"

They both shook their heads again. "Nothing," Amanda added.

"Although the group text did slow down after she got with Steve," Tiffany said with an eye roll.

"Steve's her boyfriend, right?" Adam asked. "How long have they been together?"

"It feels like an eternity to be honest with you," Amanda said, "but I think it's actually been about six months."

"Yes it has," Tiffany said, "because remember how Brooke wanted to celebrate it, and we helped her surprise him, and then he was a complete jerk about it and said six months wasn't a year so she didn't need to make a big deal about it."

"Ugh, yes. He's such a dick."

Adam glanced at Erin before he said, "Was Steve often mean to Brooke?"

Tiffany shifted uncomfortably and glanced at

Amanda. "I mean, he's just one of those guys that say dick things all the time."

"There's a fine line between being an asshole and being abusive," Erin said, and both girls looked up at her. "Did Steve ever do anything to make you worry about Brooke?"

They glanced at each other again, and then Amanda said, "Well, he can be controlling. Like he complains any time the three of us get together, and then he'll blow up her phone the whole time so it isn't even fun."

"He hates cheerleading, too," Tiffany said. "He doesn't like going to any of the games, except he also doesn't want any other guys hitting on Brooke, so then he just sits on the bleachers and glares at us like a psycho."

Amanda nodded. "He begs her to quit all the time, but so far she's resisted."

"And at parties," Tiffany said, "he always sticks right by her side so no one else can talk to her. Brooke doesn't even do anything bad at parties! No drugs, and she only drinks a beer or two." Tiffany seemed to belatedly realize she was talking to a police officer, and her eyes widened. "I mean…soda. She only had one soda."

Adam flashed a smile. "It's fine. You're not going to say anything that gets your friend in trouble. Don't worry."

"He's manipulative, too," Amanda said quietly,

fidgeting with a colorful tasseled bracelet on her arm. "One time he told Brooke that he saw us texting about her behind her back, and that we were super jealous of her and all of this stuff, but we were actually planning her birthday party."

"Yeah, we just didn't want to include *him*," Tiffany said, eyes flashing.

Manipulative guys always made Erin think of Rick, and a wave of dark regret filled her. He ranked as one of the biggest mistakes of her life, and she hated to imagine her sister with someone like that—someone pretending to love and care but who was actually deeply selfish.

"Did you ever see Brooke with bruises or marks?" Adam asked. A thick quiet descended over them, and they both wore matching looks of wide eyes and down-turned mouths. When they shook their heads, he added, "Did she ever confide in you that Steve hit her or physically harmed her in any way?"

"No," Tiffany said, "but I don't think Brooke would have stood for that."

"He just used his words to hurt her," Amanda said, pushing her hair over her shoulder in an abrupt gesture.

At first, Erin had hoped Brooke and Steve had just run away to be together. But now that she'd heard the truth from her friends, she realized that instead of it being a voluntary thing, Steve could have taken her away by force.

"Do you think Steve is capable of hurting Brooke?" Erin asked.

A pregnant pause filled the room, and Amanda's eyes filled with tears. Tiffany looked pale as she shifted in her seat. She rubbed her hand on Amanda's back for a moment before saying, "Yes. It's something we've always worried about."

"Do you think Steve is even capable of killing her?"

They both flinched, and Amanda took a shuddering breath as though holding back a flood of tears. With her hand still on her friend's back, Tiffany answered for them. "I don't know. I'm not sure of anything now."

Amanda wiped away a tear. "I honestly can't say what all he's capable of, but he's never been a good person."

Erin thought of all the happy pictures she'd seen of Brooke and Steve on Instagram. But of course she knew better than anyone how deceiving social media could be. She made her living off of it.

Even more than that, she knew what evil men were capable of.

11

Worry for Brooke hovered like a dark cloud over Erin as they returned to Adam's car. Talking to her friends had done nothing to comfort her. If anything, it had only made her suspect Steve now in the worst way. She turned to Adam, who had just turned the key in the ignition. "Steve sounds like a huge asshole. What do you know about him? Has he ever been in trouble before?"

Adam left the car in park as he answered. "He's got a few prior arrests, but nothing big or violent. He's been drunk in public before, vandalized some stuff with spray paint, and stole soda from a gas station when he was barely a teenager. No charges were ever pressed against him—seems like his dad has always come to his rescue and gotten the people affected to drop charges. From what I can tell, he's a little punk and most likely an emotionally abusive creep, but I can't find evidence of anything more than that."

Erin looked out the window at the school, thinking of everything the girls said—plus the way they kept glancing at each other. "Just because he hasn't done something in the past doesn't mean he won't do something in the future."

Adam nodded. "That's true. The past doesn't always predict future behavior. He's never been totally straight-laced, that's for sure."

"Shouldn't we go talk to his parents then? You can learn a lot about someone from their family."

Adam gave her a look. "Sure, I could speak to them again. I'm not so sure *we* should do anything though. It didn't go so well last time I took you to someone's house."

Erin let out her breath forcefully through her nose. "That was hardly my fault! Janet freaked the minute I walked in the door. It's completely different with Steve. I don't have any family history with his parents, and I really want to know more about him." She pulled her lips back in an approximation of a smile. "I'll be on my best behavior—I promise. This could be important to finding Brooke now that we know what her friends really thought of their relationship."

Adam sighed. "Fine. Just let me handle the questions."

"Sure. Although I'm pretty sure it was me who got those girls to open up about Steve just now. I don't think they would have told you what they really thought about him if I hadn't pushed."

Erin expected him to brush off her success, but he pulled his sunglasses down so she could see his eyes. "I do really appreciate that. I'm not sure they would have felt comfortable telling me that if it was just me there either." She shot him a surprised look as he put the car in reverse and headed back down the street. "All right," he said, with a sigh, "let's head to Steve's house then."

Like everything else in Huntsville, they didn't have to drive far to get where they were going. It was only five minutes and a few roads past the school before they pulled up to a blue house with a white wraparound porch and a trim yard. It wasn't quite as big as Brooke's house, but it was clearly well-taken care of.

As they walked up the driveway, Erin's phone rang. She glanced at it and saw it was Nikki. Since she knew Nikki wouldn't call unless something was literally on fire, she answered.

"Erin, I'm so sorry to do this to you," Nikki said in a rush, and in the background, Erin heard a familiar voice raising hell. "But Christopher Roland is here…"

Erin groaned. "He always has the best timing. Unfortunately for him, I'm in the middle of something and I can't talk right this second. I'll have to call back."

"What did she say?" Christopher demanded in the

background. "Tell her it is an absolute emergency! I won't be able to show my face at fashion week!"

"Do you need me to wait a minute?" Adam asked quietly. They'd both stopped on the sidewalk leading up to Steve's house.

"I'm sorry," Erin mouthed to Adam. "Nikki, how bad is the Christopher emergency on a scale of one to ten?"

Nikki snorted. "Like a negative one. I told him that you were busy with really important family stuff right now, but I agreed to see if we could catch you just chilling in the hotel for a minute."

"Yeah, well, if you could see the hotel, you'd know I wouldn't be staying in there for any length of time."

Nikki laughed. "Okay, I'll take care of this then. Sorry to bother you, boss lady."

Erin could hear her try to placate Christopher as she said, "Thanks, Nikki."

She disconnected the call right as Christopher's voice reached a tone that only dolphins could detect. Horribly, Erin barely felt any guilt over leaving him to Nikki. Mostly she just felt relief. Huntsville sucked everything out of her, and she had nothing left for the Christopher Rolands of the world.

The door opened, and a man who looked vaguely familiar stood there with a concerned frown on his face.

"Hey there, Bob," Adam said. "How are you?"

Erin flipped through her mental catalogue of people she knew from this town, knowing she'd seen this man before. It took her a moment, but honestly, all she had to do was think of the men who frequented her mother's bedroom. The years may have packed on the pounds and added wrinkles, but Erin had seen this man sneaking out of her house at night enough times to remember exactly who he was. It was the preacher, and he was—apparently—also Steve's dad.

She glared at him, arms folded across her chest as she remembered all the times he'd paid her mother for sex. And worst of all: the bruises and marks he'd left behind.

While she glared at him, Bob's face went from taken aback that a stranger was looking at him with open hostility to recognition. She saw the moment it clicked in his big, stupid head.

"What is she doing here, Detective?" he demanded.

Adam glanced at Erin in surprise. "Erin is Brooke's sister. She's concerned about her whereabouts—just like you've been worried about Steve."

Bob's gaze whipped to Adam's. "Have you found my son?"

"No, sir," Adam said, "but we wanted to ask—"

"You should be focused on finding my son—not hanging around with this jezebel. No good will come of it."

"You've got a lot of nerve," Erin said, but Bob cut her off.

"Get off my property, or I'm calling cops who will actually do their jobs."

He slammed the door in their faces, and Adam turned toward Erin, eyebrows raised. "You really know how to leave an impression."

"Yeah, well fuck him," Erin shouted loud enough to carry through the door. She kicked it too, for good measure, wishing it was his shin. How dare he treat her like *she* was the one who had sick, perverted tastes. She stalked back down the driveway, shaking in disgust.

Memories of her mother with bruises in the shape of fingers and welts from whips on her legs filled her head. He'd liked it rough, and he'd been happy to pay well for it. Just one night with him gave her mother money for rent that whole month. Janet didn't have the self-esteem to demand better, and money motivated her enough to risk her skin.

As her blood boiled over the pastor's extreme reaction, she had to stop and think why he had slammed the door in her face. Was he afraid she'd reveal all his nightly visits to Janet's house? It would be a miracle if this town didn't know about it. No doubt he still visited some poor woman at night, even if Janet had finally gotten her shit together and stopped dealing with men like him.

Then again, maybe he'd managed to keep his

darker appetites hidden from everyone. Some may have suspected that he had affairs, but maybe they didn't know he got off on hurting women. She couldn't think of a worse man to be the father of her little sister's boyfriend.

After sitting in on the interview with Brooke's friends, knowing the truth about Steve's identity only heightened her gut instinct that her sister's boyfriend couldn't be trusted.

She knew for a fact Steve's dad was a violent pervert, but what about Steve?

Like father, like son?

12

B y the time they got back to Adam's SUV, Erin had convinced herself that Steve and his abusive perverted father had done something to her beautiful baby sister. She wanted to go back to his house and scream until she went hoarse. Before she could act on the impulse, a gentle hand landed on her arm.

She looked up to find Adam watching her.

"Don't do it," he said, his tone a mixture of censure and amusement.

"Do what?"

"You have that look on your face I've seen a thousand times on the streets—like you're about to go start some shit."

Erin barked out a laugh. "Excuse me—'start some shit'?"

"You heard me. I don't know how you know Steve's dad, but it's clear the two of you were about to throw down. I'm warning you as the cop who would witness your potential assault to just save that energy for the investigation."

She held his gaze for a beat before sighing and leaning back against her seat. "Fine. Though a beat down for him has been a long time coming."

"Another preacher who doesn't live what he preaches?"

"You could say that. I don't know what Bob's like now, but all of my memories of him are absolutely horrific. Not only was he one of my mom's Johns, he also tended to get rough. I can remember bruises on her after he left."

Adam's face fell. "I'm sorry, Erin. I didn't know that part of his history. There were rumors that he slept around, but the abuse factor hasn't made it into the investigation. It could be significant, though, after what Brooke's friends told us."

Relief bloomed through Erin that they were on the same page. "Yes, that's exactly what I thought."

"Suspicious that he wanted you gone so fast, too," he added, gaze narrowed as he looked through the windshield at the house. "He's always presented himself as the polite, distraught father. It sounds like he doesn't want you showing up and revealing his dirty past."

"He's a good actor," Erin said, but before she could say more, her stomach growled loudly.

"Damn, we've got to get you something to eat—even I heard that," Adam said with a grin.

Erin laughed, feeling a slight blush rise to her cheeks. "I haven't had much of an appetite since I got here, but there is one thing I haven't had in years but still crave. Pepperoni rolls."

They were a favorite in West Virginia and the one local food Erin actually missed.

Adam groaned before nodding emphatically. "Yes. I know the best place for those, too. It's a hole in the wall, but it's a mom-and-pop Italian bakery."

"Hole in the wall restaurants are the best."

"It's settled then," Adam said and put the SUV into drive.

The bakery was exactly as described: just a little hole-in-the-wall bakery inside a small, brick building. A white sign with simple red lettering called it Mario's Italian Bakery.

"I didn't realize you meant Mario's!" Erin said, nostalgia at one of the few things she'd actually enjoyed as a teenager making her smile in anticipation.

"Best around," he said, smiling back at her. "The grease to cheese ratio is just the way I like it—dripping out of the bread."

They went inside, and the smell instantly made her salivate like she was Pavlov's dog. She closed her eyes and let the smell of yeast and cheese take her back. It wasn't that New York didn't have amazing bakeries, because of course it did, but she never let herself go to any. Food was usually just something to keep her alive and healthy rather than a substance to take pleasure in. She remembered being full and happy, without any of the ill effects eating something this greasy tended to do to you as an adult. No heartburn. No indigestion. The bakery made her think of when she used to bring Brooke here, of giggling when the cheese from their shared rolls stretched a mile from their mouths to the plate. Brooke always picked out all of the pepperonis—she said they were too spicy—but she loved the cheese and bread.

"What can I get you?" asked a pleasantly rotund woman behind the counter. When she caught site of Adam, her eyes lit up and she gave him a big smile. "Never mind—I know exactly what you'll have. Same as every other day, right?" she added with a chuckle.

He gave her an easy grin. "You know me too well."

"And what about your friend," she said with a suggestive lift of her eyebrows.

"I wouldn't dare order for her," Adam said and held out his hand for Erin to go first. "Erin, this is Martina, the owner's lovely sister. She's also the one responsible for these delicious rolls."

Martina's smile grew even wider at his praise. "Erin, it's so nice to see Adam with a friend as pretty as you. I told him it was a crime for a man as good-natured as him to be alone."

Instead of jumping to correct her about Erin, Adam said, "You're giving me too much credit, as usual."

Martina waved him off. "Your mama raised you well. Now, I know you can't argue with *that*." She turned to Erin. "What can I get for you, honey?"

"Two pepperoni rolls and a coke, please," Erin said without even thinking about it because it was the number of rolls she always ordered.

Before she could pay, Adam had already pulled out cash and handed it over to Martina. Erin glared at him when she went back to prepare their rolls.

"Hey, I had to save face in front of Martina. Do you have any idea the amount of *tsk*-ing she would have done if I let you pay?"

For once, Erin bit her tongue on a sarcastic retort. Seeing this side of Adam, one who had made friends with the local pepperoni rolls baker and treated her better than she'd seen other men treat their own family, brought a strangely warm feeling to her chest. She thought of the last date she'd gone on, where the guy had treated the waiter at the restaurant like a dog. Erin hadn't even bothered to tell him he was acting like a huge asshole. She just got up from the table and left.

Adam couldn't have been more different than every other man she'd had the misfortune of knowing.

Martina returned with piping hot rolls, smiling proudly as she handed them over. They were golden brown on the outside and full of gooey cheese and a ridiculous number of pepperonis on the inside. Erin was tempted to taste one while she was standing there waiting for Adam to get his, but she managed to rein herself in.

Outside, they found small tables and chairs with umbrellas where they could eat. They chose a table beneath a shady oak tree. Neither of them said anything to each other for a full five minutes while they devoured their first pepperoni rolls. It was even better than Erin remembered, especially since she hadn't had anything this greasy in a long time.

"Are they just like you remembered?" Adam asked after wiping grease from his hands.

"Better, actually. I can't remember who used to bake them when I came years ago—it could have been Martina—but clearly her skills have improved."

"She has a gift." He lifted his eyes heavenward as if in thanks before taking a huge bite of his second roll.

"Greasy pepperoni rolls were exactly what I needed," Erin said, taking a sip of her Coke. "I almost hate to ask, but what's the plan for the rest of the day?"

"Nothing as fun as this." He checked the time on his watch. "I'll have to go back to the station in a bit to finish up some paperwork. Later tonight I'll go to the prayer meeting at Preacher Bob's."

Erin wrinkled her nose. "What's the prayer meeting about?"

"He invited the whole town to come to his church to drive up support for everyone going out and searching for Brooke and Steve."

"Let me guess. I'm not invited."

Adam put down his roll with a grimace. "Like I said, the whole town is invited, but I don't think you should go. Not after what happened with Bob and Janet. The last thing I need is those two shutting down and refusing to tell me anything just because they have a rocky history with you."

Erin snorted. "That's hardly my fault."

"And I get that, especially after the horrible things you told me about Bob. I just don't want to put you in another position where you're having to defend yourself against accusations from when you were a teenager. Especially in front of the whole town."

Erin pushed her plate aside, suddenly not hungry anymore. "I don't need you looking out for me. I've done just fine my whole life."

"This isn't personal, Erin. In cases like this, though, it helps if you have the support of the town. If you have people actively looking for missing kids and keeping their eyes out for suspicious activity. Cops can't be everywhere at once."

Erin couldn't help but feel rejected, even though she knew he had a point. "I'm persona non grata in this town. I get it. Let's just head back to the hotel now, and maybe I can get some work done."

He finished off the last of his roll. "Do you want me to take you by the airport and get a car?"

She shook her head as she threw her uneaten roll in the trash. "I'm more comfortable walking or being driven now. I haven't driven myself anywhere in years, and I've never even owned a car." She never needed one in New York. "In fact, I think I'll just walk back to the motel from here."

Adam gestured toward his SUV, looking chagrined. "My car's right here, though. I can drop you off on my way to the station."

"No, I'm good," Erin said, waving him off as she started down the sidewalk.

She was done with this conversation, done with these people, and done with this town. But of course she couldn't leave without knowing what happened to Brooke, so that clawing, desperate feeling like she was trapped squeezed her lungs.

She shut the door of her hotel room a little harder than necessary before letting out her breath in a huff. The walk back hadn't cooled her down all the way, and it still stung that Adam had basically said she was too much trouble to bring to the prayer meeting tonight. She needed a distraction.

Halfheartedly, she pulled out her phone with the intention of checking in with Nikki. When it came to it, though, her mind balked at the idea. She could barely deal with everything going on here, much less work on top of it. The past she'd spent so much time burying sprang right to the surface here, and her anxiety made it so she always felt on the verge of a panic attack. Although he hadn't blamed her for it, Adam wasn't wrong that she elicited strong reactions from people in this town. She reminded them of their past, too—most of it seedy.

For one terrible moment, she glanced at the bottle of pills and considered knocking herself out for the rest of the day. No more memories. No more stress. Some steely part of her rebelled at the idea of giving up that easily, though. She needed to act less like the Erin who grew up here and more like the one who'd built her own business from the ground up. That Erin wouldn't be caught dead sleeping in the middle of the day. There had to be something more constructive she could do in this shitty town.

Her attention turned to the window and the ugly view outside of the parking lot and road. She could just make out the strip mall across the street from where she sat on the bed, so she moved closer. In between a title loan place and a Chinese food restaurant, she saw a tiny gym called the Huntsville Sports Center. Sports center seemed like a stretch—it barely seemed big enough to hold a bunch of treadmills—but it was a better way to pass the time than popping pills. She quickly changed into her svelte workout clothes, a calm determination already settling over her at the prospect of getting her heartrate up.

Locking the door behind her, she hurried across the street. Inside the Huntsville Sports Center, she found a small lobby with a bored-looking receptionist wearing a t-shirt with the words "gym rat" emblazoned across the chest. He perked up noticeably when he spotted Erin.

"Hey there, can I help you?"

Erin looked around at the sad gym and thought of the ones she had once belonged to in New York: multi-level, gleaming workout spaces with every possible piece of equipment she could want. This just had a small section for weight-lifting, a line of treadmills facing flat-screen TVs, and another line of stationary bikes.

"I just need a day pass," Erin said.

"A membership is our best value, and you can even do month by month if you like."

Erin smiled tightly. "Kill me if I'm still here in a month. No, I just need a quick workout while I'm in town."

He nodded. "Got it. Just passing through, right?"

"Something like that."

"That'll be ten dollars then," he said. "The day pass will get you in until midnight, and you can use all the equipment plus the showers."

"Thanks," Erin said, already eyeing the treadmills. Usually she liked stationary bikes, but she had a burning need for something higher impact. Since it was the middle of the day, no one appeared to be here so hopefully she'd have the gym to herself.

"Just let me know if you have any questions."

Erin nodded and started to walk away, but then she turned back suddenly. "Do you have a punching bag?"

"Yes, we do. It's in the room just behind the line of treadmills."

Relief spread through Erin like sinking into a warm bath. Treadmills and stationary bikes were fantastic for cardio, but sometimes she just needed to punch something.

Before she headed for the punching bag, she went to the locker room to store her gym bag. She dug through her things and removed wraps for her hands. She noted the showers the receptionist had mentioned, but they didn't look much cleaner than her hotel bathroom so she thought she might skip one here.

After locking up her things in one of the many empty lockers, she headed back to the main gym space and noticed that the receptionist was talking in a loud and animated way to another woman who was dressed to work out—well, except for the heavy makeup and styled hair. Erin shook her head once and headed into the kickboxing room. Flexing her wrapped fingers, she did a brief warmup before going at it with cross punches. Her muscles burned, and each hit into the bag was nearly as satisfying as punching the faces of all the shitty people who lived rent-free in her mind.

As soon as she'd freed herself from this miserable town and gone to college, she'd enrolled in every self-defense course she could find. She even took a gun course, but with the strict laws in New York, she'd never bothered to pursue it. Kickboxing, though, had always been her favorite.

With her upper body fully warmed up, she added in her kicks: roundhouse, side-kick, and push kicks. Then she mixed it up, combining punches and kicks at a furious pace until she poured sweat.

With endorphins flowing, a glowing happiness unfurled inside her like wings. She hadn't felt this way in days. Certainly not since Detective Herrera had broken the news about Brooke. The feeling wouldn't last long, but she'd ride the high as long as it lasted. She punched and kicked until her arms and legs wobbled, until sweat ran like a river down her back, and her chest heaved. Tonight, she'd sleep like a baby—she might not even need Xanax.

When she left the kickboxing room, she saw the receptionist still talking to the same woman, just as loudly and enthusiastically. *Well, at least her jaw is getting a good workout.*

As she walked into the locker room, dabbing sweat off the back of her neck with her towel, she paused in the entrance. A heavy steam permeated the small space, obscuring her vision and making it almost unbearably hot. "What the hell?" she muttered to herself. She heard the showers running, and so she went to see why so many people had decided to take the hottest showers imaginable all at the same time. When she turned the corner, she saw that all of the curtains were pulled back from the stalls. Not only were they empty, but each faucet had the hot water turned onto max. This pumped a torrent of steam into the room, turning the small area into a sauna.

Was that the point, maybe? The gym wouldn't shell out for an actual sauna, so they turned their locker room into one? But then why hadn't the receptionist mentioned it before?

She walked toward each faucet and turned it off with efficient movements, but the hair on the back of her neck stood up. With the low lighting and thick, vision-obstructing steam, the room had taken on a horror-movie feel.

As the steam began to clear, she noticed a pile of cloth on the floor. She moved closer and could just make out letters that spelled NYC on a tank top. With a furrowed brow and slightly shaky hands, she picked it up. It was definitely her top. How had it gotten on the floor? Did she drop it without realizing? But she'd never even opened her gym bag in here.

She scanned the floor in front of the lockers and froze when she saw a glint of metal. She'd recognize that metal keychain anywhere—she'd bought it from her college gift shop and had carried it ever since. She snatched it up, muscles tense and ears straining for any telltale signs that someone hid in this locker room with her.

Just one more thing laid on the floor in front of the lockers: her wallet. Her mouth went dry as she picked it up and hurriedly flipped through its contents. All there. Even the three hundred dollars in cash.

She looked up at the locker where she'd put her things, the third from the top. The door stood slightly ajar, and Erin's fingers trembled as she opened it all the way. Her bag sat where she'd left it. Heart in her throat, she rifled through the contents. As expected, her tank top, keys, and wallet were missing, and as she put them back in the bag, she groaned in horror when she realized what else had been taken: a pair of plain black panties.

With jerky movements, she searched the entirety of the locker room. Her panties were nowhere to be found.

Her heart pounded painfully as she clutched her

bag to her chest. Who did this? What did it mean? She had to get the fuck out of there.

Erin slammed the locker shut and whirled toward the door, but as she passed by the mirrors, she stopped dead. A message waited on one of the mirrors, written in steam. The letters were scrawled in an ugly script, but she had no trouble reading them. She pressed her fingers to her mouth to stifle a scream as her eyes scanned and rescanned the message waiting for her:

Welcome home.

13

THEN

The hard, wooden pew creaked under Erin as she squirmed in her seat, drawing disapproving stares from the old women in front of her. She knew she should stop giving them an excuse to glare at her, but honestly, they'd do it anyway now that the rumors had spread.

Erin glanced over at her mom, who sat next to Brooke in a daze. Whatever she'd smoked and drank last night hadn't worn off yet. Brooke colored in her little book, and Erin smiled despite herself at her innocence. Had Erin ever been that innocent? Had Janet allowed her to be? And now look at her life. It was a complete train wreck after what happened last week at school.

The principal had ended up calling Janet, and for once Erin was glad she was high. She came to the school only after the principal threatened to get the police involved. So Janet came and sat with the same stupid look she had on her face now. She didn't appear to give a shit when the principal detailed what he'd walked in on. That her daughter was engaged in sexual activity with a much older—and married—teacher.

"I hope he paid you good," was all she said. Erin cringed and squirmed again to think of it.

Erin's biggest fear, though, wasn't her reputation. The thought that social services would finally get involved and take Brooke away kept her up late at night. In the end, though, the school didn't report any of it. The principal fired Rick and told Erin he didn't want the school being dragged through the mud just because she was a slut.

Fine by Erin. It was better not to get authorities involved. She couldn't risk them taking her baby sister away, and she didn't want anything affecting her college applications either.

But just because no legal action was being taken didn't mean the gossip hadn't already spread from one corner of Huntsville to another.

Behind her, old Mrs. Jackson came and sat down beside her lifelong friend, Mrs. Williamson. In the whole church, and maybe the whole town, these two women had always been kind to Erin. They always asked about her schoolwork, and when she was younger, used to bring her little treats after church. She thought of them like Sunday grandmothers—when Janet let them go to church, anyway.

So when Mrs. Jackson sat down, Erin turned around with a smile. But instead of smiling back and leaning forward to talk to Erin, Mrs. Jackson's face twisted in something that was perilously close to disgust. She turned to Mrs. Williamson like she hadn't seen Erin at all. Mrs. Williamson, too, seemed to be pointedly ignoring Erin.

Erin jerked back around like she'd been slapped. Tears pricked her eyes.

Before she lost control and started sobbing in front of everyone—wouldn't they all love that?—Erin hurried out of her pew and practically ran to the bathroom.

All Erin wanted to do was get to a stall so she could cry in peace, but the moment she walked in the brightly-lit bathroom with its ugly yellow wallpaper, she was met by a woman washing her hands at the sink. When her gaze lifted to meet Erin's in the mirror, Erin's heart sank. It was Rick's wife, Norma. She couldn't think of a worse person to run into.

Norma's hair was teased so high it made her look six feet tall, and she used every inch of her height advantage to turn around and tower over Erin. "I can't believe you would even show your face here."

"At church? I thought all were welcome," Erin said with a sarcastic bite that she didn't truly feel.

"Well that doesn't apply to trash like you," she said with a sneer. "You know Rick lost his job because of you? Now no one will hire him. He'll never teach again, and he had a real calling. He was a real good teacher. All the kids loved him, but I guess you just loved him too much."

Erin could barely look her in the eyes, and she certainly couldn't come up with a response. It turned out she didn't need to, though. Norma had something to say, and she was going to make sure Erin listened.

"We got kids, you know," she said, her tone becoming more incensed. "Rick told me you stupidly thought he was going to leave me and my babies and run off with you." She laughed cruelly. "He's a respectable family man. Not some loser who would leave for a floozy like you." She leaned closer, poking Erin in the chest. "You're a whore. Just like your mama."

The last poke came with a shove, and Erin stumbled back. Norma left the bathroom, head held high.

When she was finally alone, Erin crumpled to the floor, sobs overtaking her.

Erin finally peeled herself off the floor of the bathroom and slipped back into her pew just as Preacher Bob started his sermon. She thought about hiding in the bathroom the rest of the time, but she worried about someone else coming in, and she didn't want to leave Brooke alone with their mother. She was too hungover to be trusted to watch her baby sister.

Erin avoided looking at anyone and just concentrated on little Brooke, who was still quietly coloring. The preacher droned on, but when he suddenly mentioned the sins of women, Erin tensed.

"As you know, the fall of mankind was due to the sins of a woman. She took the fruit from the devil himself, but you know that didn't just mean a harmless little apple like you'd get from the market. No, no. The real sin was that Eve slept with the devil, opening herself up to the first carnal sins."

Erin looked around at the nodding heads, confusion slowing her thoughts. Slept with the devil? She was pretty sure she never heard this version in Sunday school.

"And then Eve passed on her knowledge of carnal pleasures to Adam so that they were both ashamed of their nakedness and even tried to hide from God. And who did Eve bear after that sexual encounter with the devil? It was Cain! Cain, the first murderer.

"We see time and again in the Bible that women are sinful creatures, constantly tempting men and bringing about their downfall. What about Jezebel? What about Delilah? The Bible is full of harlots and other female sinners, and it makes it deadly clear that such behavior cannot be tolerated. We need to show these sinners that we won't stand for such scandalous acts—not at our church!"

His voice reverberated across the small congregation, and the whispers and stares started almost immediately after. Erin caught her name many times, as well as her mother's. She sank down lower in the pew and rubbed her chest like a red "A" was emblazoned there. Preacher Bob was up there pointing out the sins of her family, even though he'd participated in them. He hadn't meant that sermon to include himself, though—she knew he thought he was exempt. No doubt he blamed it on her mother "tempting" him into sinning. Erin twisted her skirt in her hands. A scream built inside her, and for a horrible moment, she pictured herself letting loose on everyone here. What would they all do then? But she glanced at Brooke, so sweet and innocent, and the urge passed.

After a few more hymns and more thinly-veiled stares, the service was finally over, and Erin could escape. She gathered up Brooke's things and tried to hurry their mother along. Before they could even leave the pew, though, Preacher Bob was there.

"I wanted to speak to you in case you didn't listen to my sermon," he said, his face smug. "This church can no longer tolerate such blatant sinfulness—not only from you, Janet, but from Erin, too. It scandalizes the faithful and makes it hard for everyone to concentrate on God's word." Janet watched him with hooded eyes and a slight smile, and Erin could tell she thought she was giving him a seductive look. Erin held Brooke closer to her side, praying she didn't understand what was going on.

"Do you understand what I'm saying to you, Janet?" Preacher Bob said sharply. "Your family is no longer welcome here."

It seemed to take Janet a moment to comprehend his words, but when she did, her face darkened into a look Erin knew all too well.

"*You're* kicking me out?" she demanded. "After all we've *shared* together?" She made a rude gesture toward her breasts and lower half, and the eavesdroppers nearby gasped. Preacher Bob turned bright red, but whether it was from embarrassment or rage was hard to tell.

"You absolutely reek, Janet," Preacher Bob said. "I can smell the alcohol on your breath."

At some point, Norma had joined the eavesdroppers. Now she took her chance to further humiliate them. "What kind of person comes to church drunk?"

"Someone who doesn't belong here," Preacher Bob said.

All around them, the crowd of churchgoers nodded and murmured their assent. So many of them had disgusted looks on their faces that Brooke burst into tears. Erin pulled her closer to her side. "Mama, let's just leave," she said, shame eating at her like a poison.

"All y'all can burn in Hell," Janet said and whirled away. Or at least she tried to. She was so unsteady from the alcohol that she stumbled and almost fell. Cruel laughs followed them out the church doors.

Just as they reached the sidewalk to head back home, a man called out to them. Erin wanted to ignore him, but Janet turned. She could never resist a man who wanted to talk to her.

He loped over to them, his body skeletal. At first, Erin thought he might be one of the homeless men who came to the church pantry for help with food. His long, shabby hair fell in his face, and his clothes were old and tattered. When he got closer to them, the first thing Erin noticed about his face was his bright red nose full of burst capillaries—the hallmark of a raging alcoholic like Janet.

"I couldn't help but overhear what happened in there," he said with a sympathetic look. "I volunteer at the church as a janitor, so I was in the back cleaning." He held his mop up as if in explanation. Erin didn't recognize him from the service, but he pulled a little cart behind him full of cleaning supplies. "They got meetings in the community center across the street there—every Monday and Wednesday. You should come. I haven't touched a drop in over a month now, so I know what it's like. These meetings could save your life."

Hope soared inside Erin. This could be exactly what Janet needed. She tried for a moment to imagine her mother completely sober, but she struggled to produce even a fleeting image in her mind. Her mother never had anyone try to help her before, though. Maybe all she needed was some encouragement and accountability. The man caught Erin's gaze and smiled as though he sensed her hopefulness.

Erin smiled back tentatively before turning to her mother. "Mama, maybe you should go to those meetings."

Her mother's alcohol-soaked brain seemed to churn through the information slowly, but then she sneered. "Those are for alcoholics." She pointed at the man, who just watched her with a kind look on his face. "What you overheard was a bunch of lies by a very sick man. The preacher should be ashamed of himself—treating me like that in front of my girls."

He nodded before loading his mop into the cart, too. "Well, if you ever want to join us, it's open to everyone."

Please, Mama, Erin thought, but she didn't say it. It

would only make Janet double-down on her insistence that she didn't have a problem.

With her head held high, Janet turned away from the man, giving Brooke's hand a little tug. She walked away, stumbling a bit on the uneven sidewalk.

"Thanks for trying to help," Erin said to him, her face growing warm as she turned to follow her mother and sister.

"Any time," he called after her.

14

NOW

By the time Erin got back to her dingy hotel room, she was shaking violently. She searched every inch of the small room and bathroom, every hair on her arms and back of her neck standing on end. After double-checking the locked door, she took a shower so fast she barely washed all the shampoo out of her hair. Every second she pictured the scene from *Psycho* and kept having to pull aside the curtain to check.

She knew she'd looked a little unhinged when she left the gym. The receptionist had called out a cheery good-bye as she walked toward the door, but his happy smile had instantly fallen away when he saw Erin's face. She didn't bother to explain or ask any questions. She just hurried out of there like she'd robbed a bank.

Questions swirled in her head like a whirling tornado of leaves. What did the message mean? When she thought about the locker room with its thick steam that could have hidden anyone in it, and the trail of her things on the floor like a crime scene, her hands started shaking so badly she had to hold them to stop it. Despite the words of the message, whoever wrote it didn't want her to feel welcomed home. Was this connected to Brooke somehow?

She paced as she thought, her hand on her ever-tightening chest. Did someone want to try and scare her off and send her home before she could really help Adam investigate? But who would do that? An image of Bob slamming the door in her face filled her mind. He certainly seemed capable of trying to scare her off, but in all her experience with him, he seemed to prefer to tell her in person.

Her own mother had practically thrown Erin out of her house, but could she have snuck down to the gym and left a message like that, knowing Erin would find it deeply disturbing? Erin would have laughed if her heart wasn't galloping away in her chest like a runaway horse. No, Janet was many things, but subtle wasn't one of them.

Then who? Someone random who just wanted to play a prank? There were plenty of people in this town who had never liked Erin—she had no delusions about that. Sweat beaded her hairline as she thought. The t-shirt she'd pulled over her head after her shower was already uncomfortably damp in places.

The thought came, then, that made her legs quiver with weakness: what if it was *him*? What if he had Brooke and wanted to send Erin a message?

She shook her head so violently it strained her neck. *No.* No, she couldn't entertain thoughts like that. Monsters from thirteen years ago didn't suddenly resurface. What would the chances of that be?

Now that the thought had entered her head, though, cold fingers traced their way down her spine. She should have never come. Why had she thought she could be any help in a missing-person investigation? Things hadn't gone well since she arrived—everyone she met reacted to her with naked hostility. And now this. It made her want to book the next flight out of town.

But as she paced around, she thought of Brooke. She couldn't abandon her here—again. The whole reason she'd agreed to come back to this godforsaken place was to help her baby sister in any way she could. She just hadn't factored in this level of emotional trauma resurfacing. Almost against her will, her gaze found the bottle of Xanax again.

She considered the night ahead of her. She could sit here and work herself into a panic attack that someone could break into her motel room, and then take a bunch of Xanax and pass out. Or she could contact Detective Herrera and let him know what happened. They'd been on the same page about Bob's reaction to her, so she didn't think he would dismiss it as paranoia.

She stood up and grabbed her purse, only to remember he said he'd be at the church prayer meeting that night. He'd made it clear he didn't want her to go, but he needed to know what happened. She pulled out her phone and brought up the detective's contact info. Before she pressed send, though, she thought about who might be at that church meeting. What if the person who left her that message was there? She could go and observe how everyone reacted to her...see if there was anyone who seemed like they might be responsible for scaring the shit out of her today.

Her mind made up, she slipped her phone back into her purse. Better to ask forgiveness than permission, so she would just walk the couple of blocks to the church and brazen it out. She quickly changed into nicer clothes—a tailored black dress and heels.

The moment she stepped out of the relative safety of her motel room again, her whole body tensed. What if whoever left her that message was watching her right now? The street seemed empty save for a few passing cars, but that didn't mean someone wasn't looking at her from inside one of the strip mall stores.

Pinpricks ran down her spine, and it became a little harder to draw a breath. Still, she forced herself forward, desperately missing the anonymity of a big city like New York.

I know how to defend myself, she repeated in her mind, but the band around her chest didn't loosen.

She picked up her pace, and by the time she saw the brick church in the distance, she'd rendered her shower pointless. Sweat poured from every inch of her. She had to stop and run into a little coffee shop to use the bathroom there. When she saw herself in the mirror, she sighed. Her hair had escaped the bun she'd put it in, and her dress stuck to her because of the sweat. She smoothed her hair back into shape, mopped up the sweat with paper towels, and reapplied antiperspirant. Her makeup hadn't budged because she always used waterproof everything to deal with the nervous sweat.

Back on the sidewalk, it took only a few minutes of walking before sweat beaded along her hairline again. The back of her neck prickled, and she kept checking behind her as she approached the church's main entrance.

An arctic blast from air conditioning working overtime hit her when she stepped inside, and she just stood there for a moment, letting it cool her down. The lobby was clear of people, but posters and pamphlets with Brooke and Steve's smiling faces were placed at regular intervals. She could hear Preacher Bob's booming voice over the state-of-the-art sound system, and it was obvious the sleazy preacher had done well for himself. With updated lighting, new flooring, and a much bigger space, she could tell the church building had been renovated. When she entered the main sanctuary, she noticed that the old wooden pews were gone. In their place were heavily padded chairs, and almost all of them were full. It took her a moment to find Adam in the crowd, but then she saw him close to the front.

It seemed like the entire town was here, listening intently to Preacher Bob's opening prayer. Erin had to stifle a gag as he theatrically lifted his eyes heavenward and raised his arms.

"Father God, we come to ask for your blessing and guidance tonight. Only you know how much our hearts cry out for the missing children, Brooke and Steve," he said, and though he let emotion creep into his tone at the mention of his son's name, Erin also knew he adored the sound of his own voice. It reverberated perfectly inside the space, with speakers to make sure it reached every corner. She wondered if Steve was like his father: arrogant and narcissistic. Those were traits of an abuser, and from what

Brooke's friends said, Steve likely fell into that category.

The prayer continued for at least five minutes, until Erin could no longer fight the drag of memories on her mind. She thought of the last time she'd been in church with Brooke and Janet. She thought of how horribly they were treated by people pretending to be God-fearing Christians. Brooke had just been a little girl then, yet they'd humiliated her mother and sister in front of her. Now some of those same people were here, pretending to be worried to death over Brooke's missing status.

"I'm going to invite my fellow parents and the sheriff to say a few words," Preacher Bob said, finally ending his long-winded prayer. Janet and Phil were quick to join him next to the pulpit. But the moment Erin saw the sheriff, her whole body blazed with an anger she hadn't thought about in a long, long time.

It was Sheriff Holland, the same good old boy who not only didn't believe her about her kidnapping, but went out of his way to declare her a liar. Even to her own mother.

If it turned out that Brooke had been kidnapped, would he believe *her*?

Maybe it was because she was in the back thrumming with anger, but suddenly, Adam's eyes scanned the crowd of people behind him. Eventually, he landed on her. While Sheriff Holland cleared his throat and addressed the crowd, Adam got out of his seat and came to her side.

"Are you allergic to doing what someone asks you to do or what?" Adam said, keeping his voice low. Erin bristled at his scolding tone, which combined with the sheriff up there pretending to care about people, grated her raw.

"I have good reason to be here," she said tightly. She didn't want to get into what happened to her while she was trying to hear what they all said about Brooke, so she left it at that.

Adam searched her face, but she kept her focus on the pulpit. Sheriff Holland looked like hell. An enormous belly hung over the waist of his pants, making him at least two sizes bigger than he'd been when she was a teenager. Even from the back of the room, she noticed the mess of broken capillaries and deep furrows of his face. His hair—never much to begin with—now looked wispy and sad.

"Just try to keep a low profile," Adam said, and she scoffed.

When he gave her a pointed look and gestured toward a poster of Brooke, she rolled her eyes. "Fine. I won't go picking a fight." That didn't mean she wouldn't finish one though.

Detective Herrera sighed and nodded, and they both refocused on what the sheriff was saying.

"We are asking that anyone who has information

on Brooke and Steve—strange social media posts, text messages, or even overheard conversations—come forward immediately. If you've seen something, even something as simple as them talking to someone you didn't recognize or even driving together in Steve's car on the day of their disappearance, we need you to let the police know. It could be vital to our investigation."

His eyes swept over the crowd. "You know, we're a small community here in Huntsville. That means we take care of our own. And right now, two of our kids are missing. We've got to come together and do everything we can to find them—leave no rock unturned."

Erin sucked in her breath at his words. Pain and anger rushed through her like a spreading fire. Where was this "community" when she was kidnapped? No one set up a prayer meeting for her or organized a search party. The sheriff didn't believe her, and he made sure everyone knew that she was just some lying, manipulative girl—like her mother. Erin had suspected it was because the sheriff couldn't easily solve the case. He didn't believe girls like her could escape a kidnapping situation. And he'd led everyone else in town to believe the same. Many of the same people were here today, only older. They gripped each other's hands and looked around the room with worried expressions. They appeared to deeply care that Brooke and Steve were missing, and Erin couldn't help but wonder if that was because they came from different families than

Erin. Janet was her mother, too, but the Janet of her teenage years was nothing like this sober, put-together woman who stood in front of everyone. Janet of the past wouldn't have even showed up for her own daughter's prayer meeting. It helped to have a well-dressed husband beside her, who gave her a sense of legitimacy for the shallow people of this town.

Sheriff Holland finally finished his bullshit buttering-up of this "tight-knit" community, and then Janet stepped up to the pulpit. Even from the back of the room, Erin could tell her eyes welled up with tears. Her bottom lip quivered as she shakily adjusted the mic.

"My daughter, Brooke," she said, and then immediately burst into tears.

All around the room came sympathetic murmurs as Phil stepped forward to rub Janet's back. Janet took a moment to calm down, dabbing at her eyes with a tissue.

She took a shaky breath before continuing. "I'm sorry. This is so hard. So many of you know and love Brooke," she said, and Erin saw many in the crowd nod. "She always has a kind word for everyone, and she likes to be involved in our little town. She loves being on the cheer squad, and she plays the violin beautifully. Her friends mean everything to her." Here Janet gave a tearful smile to Brooke's friends and their families. Erin recognized Amanda and Tiffany, both sitting with their parents and siblings. There were others, too. Several rows of teenagers and their families, many of whom were crying.

"Her room always looks like a tornado hit it because she likes to try on so many different outfits before finding the perfect one. She has big plans to go to college and major in fashion design. She's an early riser, and when she gets up, she always fixes her stepdad and me a fresh cup of coffee so it's ready when we finally roll out of bed." Janet gave a sad little laugh and glanced at Phil, who reached out and held her hand. "She's my little girl, and I love her so much. She's the kindest person I know, and that's why I'm begging all of you to help us. Help us bring our girl home."

Janet's words were honest and heartfelt, and emotion stirred deep inside Erin. Not only did she not recognize this version of Janet, but she also didn't know this Brooke. The four-year-old who used to curl up and sleep at the diner while Erin worked was gone, replaced by this shining example of American wholesomeness. And Erin missed all of it. She'd been so busy trying to create the perfect life for herself that she completely missed out on Brooke's.

At least Janet had made one thing clear: Brooke's life was nothing like Erin's. The guilt of leaving Brooke behind to be raised by Janet had always been a painful wound that had never scarred over completely. But by some miracle, Janet had clearly gotten her life together.

She'd sobered up, gotten married to Phil, and actually given Brooke a normal childhood.

Somewhere deep inside Erin, a new sensation came to life that she tried to ignore. A strange, festering feeling of envy and resentfulness. Janet hadn't deemed Erin important enough to change her life for. Erin never got this new Janet as a mother, and it hurt. Bad.

Janet ended her speech with another heartfelt plea for God's intervention and help finding her daughter, and then Phil took her place at the pulpit. His eyes were red-rimmed and his voice shook as he spoke about Brooke.

"I may not be Brooke's biological father, but I've been blessed to be able to help raise her. I love that girl like she was my own. She's beautiful inside and out, and we just need her to come home. We're organizing a search party for Brooke tomorrow, and it would mean the world to her mother and me if you could come." He broke down for a moment and wiped his face with his hand. "Please help us find our little girl and Steve," he managed to get out before turning into Janet's waiting arms.

Erin watched Janet pat his broad back, tears pricking her eyes. Talk of search parties reminded her that it had been another day with no sign of Brooke. If *he* really did take her, then Erin knew what that meant. She remembered what happened on the fifth day. How things went from bad to worse and didn't stop until she escaped. It changed the course of her entire life, but that was only because she made it out alive. What if Brooke didn't? What if she was already dead? A sob caught in her throat, and she instinctively reached out for human contact. Adam's hand was warm and strong. He glanced down at her and gave her hand a squeeze as they watched on.

15

E rin mumbled an excuse to Adam about needing to use the restroom, but really she needed a break from the endless emotional turmoil that emanated in that room. As she walked toward the bathroom, she couldn't help but think of the time Norma cornered her and blamed her for her husband's disgusting behavior.

Norma may not have been there, but there was a group of women gossiping outside the bathroom. Erin started to excuse herself and walk by them, but then she caught the name Brooke and paused.

"It's sad about Brooke and all," one woman said, folding her arms across her ample chest, "but I just couldn't stomach hearing Janet act like she's some sort of upstanding member of society now."

There was a chorus of "uh huhs" because the

others weren't capable of coming up with anything more creative.

"She's the most uppity piece of trash—ever since she married Phil. As if him being the head of the community center is that big a deal." She rolled her eyes theatrically, and the others laughed. "She needs to remember her place, honestly. She's always been a trashy whore, even if she tries to dress and act nice now."

Erin's hands curled into fists at her sides, and she itched to smack the sneer off her face. Who did these bitches think they were? She moved closer and suddenly it hit her: she knew them. They looked completely different now than they did in high school, but Erin couldn't forget her high school bully Stephanie and her two lemming friends. Instead of her once long and beautiful hair, Stephanie sported a severe bob that only highlighted her round face and double chin. Her youthful skin had turned wrinkled and haggard, and she'd traded in her stylish clothes for a frumpy church lady suit and sensible pumps. The other two had similarly unflattering looks, like they all shopped at the Dress Barn together and went to the same unfortunate hairdresser.

Erin could have looked past all of that—even though it was seriously good karma—except their conversation revealed who they really were. They clearly had never grown out of the nasty, cruel comments they'd made in high school.

Stephanie still hadn't noticed Erin, being far too busy spewing nasty hate to her little entourage of lemmings. It was one thing for Erin to talk badly about Janet, but she'd earned that right after years of neglect. Stephanie hadn't earned shit.

Erin strode toward the three of them, these pathetic women who used to rule the school, and now who just looked dumpy compared to Erin's sleek, tailored dress, sky-high heels, and perfect makeup. She was the City Girl to their Country, and she wasn't afraid to shove it in their faces.

Erin didn't hesitate. She marched right into the midst of them and took up their space. When they caught sight of her, they physically stepped back.

"You know, it's funny you were talking about someone needing to be put in her place just now," Erin said with her coldest smile. "I feel like that's been a long time coming for you, Stephanie."

It took Stephanie a moment or two, but then she said, "Erin?" Erin responded by crossing her arms and arching her brow. "Wow, I'd love to hear how someone like *you* could put *me* in my place."

The other two snickered, and it was just like being in high school again. Except this time, Erin most definitely had the upper hand.

"Well, while the three of you were stuck in this hellhole of a town, evidently getting fat and old, I actually went out and made something of myself. I have my own PR business in New York City that represents fashion designers like Christopher Roland." Erin paused and took in their outfits slowly, a smirk on her face. Stephanie's face bloomed bright red under her scrutiny. "It's obvious from what you're wearing that you have no idea who I'm talking about. And for you to make fun of my mother, who managed to better herself even while living in this backwards town, is the most pathetic thing I've ever heard. All of you peaked in high school, and the people you spent all your time looking down on have actually risen above you."

Stephanie's mouth opened and closed and her eyes were as wide as a doe's. She sputtered a few times and managed a weak, "Fuck you, Erin."

Erin just laughed. After such a delicious reaction, she no longer felt the need to waste time in the bathroom. She turned on her heel and returned to Adam's side, buoyed by finally being able to tell off her high school bullies. There was nothing like sweet revenge to chase away any other stress or painful emotions, and for about five minutes, Erin's spirits rose.

But then Sheriff Holland marched over to Adam, his bulldog face ruddy. Every muscle in Erin's body stiffened. He grabbed Adam by the arm and pulled him aside.

"Where the hell do you get off thinking you could

go to Bob's house with *her*?" He stabbed a meaty finger in Erin's direction, and her fists curled at her sides. "Do you want my biggest donor thinking we're not taking this case seriously? Because that's what it looks like when you bring a liar like her around with you. I can't have you upsetting Bob like that when his only son is missing!"

"A liar? Sir, I've been looking at old cases of missing persons, and—"

"Why are you looking at old cases? We haven't even solved this one! I want you in my office first thing tomorrow morning." He turned to Erin, grizzled brows drawn low over his small eyes. "You're going to have to go back to whatever big city you flew in from. Word is, you've done nothing but stir up trouble since you got here. Things would go a lot smoother if you left. Tonight."

There was a time when Erin would have been intimidated, but that was when she was seventeen years old. Now she knew he was full of shit. "Are you going to arrest me if I don't?" When his face turned more thunderous, she added, "I've got a question for you, Sheriff. Were you near the Huntsville Sports Center this afternoon?"

His wiry eyebrows drew low over his piggish eyes in what was either a look of confusion or anger. "Just stay out of the way and don't get involved in my case.

Herrera shouldn't have brought you here," he added with another fat finger stab toward Adam.

He may not have revealed much when she asked him about the gym, but his reaction to Erin told her that the sheriff should be added to her mental list of suspects. He had never treated her right, not even when she was a desperate teenager in need of help, so it came as no surprise that he acted like a raging asshole now.

Memories of the last time she'd seen the sheriff threatened to overcome her:

His sneer as he refused to help.

The nonchalance pouring from his body as he casually destroyed any hope she'd held of justice.

His body may have changed, but he shot her the exact same look of disdain he'd given her as a teenager. He strode away before either of them could respond, disgustingly sure that he would be obeyed.

Well, he had another thing coming.

16

A fter the prayer meeting and the way Sheriff Holland had shown his back to both of them, Adam's expression had darkened like a sudden storm. A muscle in his jaw repeatedly flexed like he was gritting his teeth, and his neck and shoulders were tense. She could certainly empathize. Sheriff Holland had always pissed her off, too. She couldn't believe he was still sheriff here after all these years.

As she stood beside Adam, waves of anger coming off him like a furnace, she sensed something strange within herself. All her life, even before her kidnapping, she'd often had full-blown panic attacks whenever a man became angry around her. Janet never brought home nice guys, and they frequently filled the house not only with raised voices but also violence.

She stole a glance at him. He still held his body

rigidly straight, but instead of her usual instinct to get away, she wanted to reach out to him. Even though she hadn't known Adam long, no warnings bells that he would take out his anger on her went off.

So it was with these thoughts in mind that she suddenly blurted, "Hey, you wanna go somewhere? Like get a drink or something?"

He looked at her in surprise, some of the tension momentarily leaving his face. After a moment's consideration, he nodded. "I think we both could use a drink."

There was a bar only a block over from the church, and Erin thought it must be new since she didn't remember it from her years here. Growing up with Janet ensured she knew every bar in town. This one was called Smiley's and had a whole lot of neon signage, a big bar made of copper, a couple of pool tables, and plenty of dim lighting. The best part, though, was that she didn't see anyone she recognized inside.

She and Adam chose a table in a back corner, far from the pool tables.

"Can I get you something from the bar?" Adam asked.

"Yes, but I'm paying."

Adam leveled his gaze at her. "I can tell you're used to getting your way in stuff like this, but you should know, I'm not going to budge. So just give up and let me buy you a drink."

She normally would have insisted—she didn't like to owe other people—but then she decided to give in for once. See what it was like to have someone pay for her for a change. "Fine," she said with a weary smile. "I'll have a whiskey sour."

He smacked his hand on the table before standing up. "Good choice."

There weren't many people at the bar, so he returned with her drink and a beer for him before she could even finish reading one of her many neglected emails.

"Thank you," Erin said, taking a sip. "I don't normally drink, but today was rough."

"It really has been one shitstorm after another," Adam said with a long pull of his beer. "Holland's had it out for me ever since this investigation started, so I guess I shouldn't be surprised he decided to show his ass at a prayer meeting."

"That's just Holland being Holland. He hasn't changed since I was a teenager."

She swirled the ice in her drink around and looked up to find Adam watching her.

"I heard you ask Holland about being near the gym this afternoon. What was that about?"

"That's actually why I came to the prayer meeting. I wanted to tell you what happened, but then I didn't get the chance. I was the only person in the gym today, but when I got done working out, all the showers were turned on to full blast. It was so hot and steamy in the locker room I could hardly see. When I turned them off, there was a message on the mirror directly across from my locker that said, 'Welcome home.'"

Adam's brows were drawn low over his eyes. "Damn, Erin. You must have been terrified." His tone was serious, and a wave of relief hit Erin. She didn't realize how scared she was that he wouldn't believe her until she finally told him.

"That wasn't the only thing. Someone left a trail of my stuff—my workout top, my wallet—and left my locker door ajar. But when I checked my bag, everything was there, even the contents of my wallet. Everything except a pair of underwear."

His jaw tightened. "They were trying to screw with your head. Are you sure you were alone at the gym? What about the receptionist?"

"Before I even went in to work out, the receptionist was talking with this other woman. They seemed deep in conversation—laughing and cutting up—and they were still talking when I came out of the kickboxing room."

"And you didn't recognize either of them?"

She shook her head. "The woman was dressed to work out, but she obviously just came there to gossip with the receptionist. They looked like old friends."

Adam stared at his beer thoughtfully. "In a strip mall like that, each store would have its own back entrance, so someone could have slipped in the back door. It would have to be someone watching you to know you were even there though. That's what really bothers me."

Erin took a bigger sip of her whiskey. "I fucking hate this town."

"I thought I would, too, but it grew on me. At least until this recent kidnapping case where I'm the only one doing any actual investigating."

"I can't say I'm surprised. The cops here have always been shit. What are the others doing if not helping find my sister?"

"You saw it tonight—they're trying to round up people in town to help search. To them, it's a missing persons case. They're not convinced it's a kidnapping case, and they're sure as hell not buying my hunch that it could be the work of a serial kidnapper."

Erin leaned back in her seat with a huff. "That's exactly what I was afraid of. The cops in this town—present company excluded—have never wanted to do their job."

Adam held his beer glass in mock salute. "Good to know. I just thought the others had it out for me. They haven't liked my ideas since day one."

"Now that's crazy. Working a precinct in Chicago should give you some clout. I can almost guarantee none of them have anywhere near the same experience as you."

He smirked at his glass. "It's nice to hear Chicago just roll off your lips like that. Some of the guys I work with have turned it into a slur. 'No one asked for your advice, *Chicago*. That's not how we do things around here.'"

She shook her head. "I think it's something in the water that makes all the people in this town assholes." After taking another drink, she gave him a pointed look. "Are you finally going to let me in on what brought you to this hellscape from Chicago?"

He took a big swig of his beer. "That's going to require another drink. Same again?"

She shook her glass and finished the last of the whiskey. "Okay, but this is the last round you're paying for."

He waved her off and went to get their drinks. When he returned, he pulled his chair a little closer to hers. She didn't even lean away.

"It doesn't seem like it now, but I was a hotshot detective in Chicago. Or at least I thought I was. I had a run of successful cases solved—murder happens every day in that city, so if you've got good instincts, you can rocket your career in no time. But that also contributed to me thinking I was the shit when I'd honestly just solved cases that had the evidence practically wrapped up with a bow."

"You sound like you're selling yourself short. You convinced me to fly all the way here, after all."

He smiled at that, but it didn't reach his eyes. "Actually, I don't think I've been hard enough on myself. That's why I couldn't overlook this possible lead in your sister's case. It hasn't been an easy, open-and-shut one like those first cases I had in Chicago."

"What made them easy?"

"They were crimes of passion, so the murderers in all the cases confessed after barely any pressure. I convinced myself it was because of my superior detective skills, though, so when a serial killer case came up, I volunteered." He took a swig of his beer and pulled a face like it was bitter, but Erin thought it was more due to the memories he was dredging up.

"Serial—you used that word before. You said you thought Brooke might be the victim of a serial kidnapper."

"It's a word we don't like to hear on an investigation, and that may be why the others on my force don't want to entertain that possibility." He caught and held her gaze, his expression turning sympathetic. "I don't want to use that term when I talk about your sister's case, either—believe me."

Erin swallowed hard. She could barely think of the possibility that her sister may have been kidnapped, much less by some psycho who'd taken and killed other girls. "When you were in Chicago, though, you didn't mind taking a serial killer case?"

He scoffed. "That's because I thought—wrongly—that I was the best of the best."

"What happened?"

He shot her a self-deprecating smile. "I screwed up. Bad. I came up with a suspect right away, and I hounded this guy. I was convinced he was our killer. Everything in me told me this was the guy—he had a creepy wall of newspaper clippings, he'd been in the area of the killings, and he was sketchy as hell—but while I was obsessed with nailing that guy, the real killer murdered again." He hunched his shoulders like the memory pained him.

Erin reached out and touched his arm. "That's terrible, but it's not like you're psychic—you were just following a lead."

"I was blindly following the wrong lead, though. It was my fault that my tunnel vision made me miss key signs, like the fact that my suspect was autistic who belonged to one of those online murder-mystery solving groups. You know the ones? They get together online and try and solve real-life crimes. The irony is that the guy told me what kind of suspect I should be looking for, but of course I didn't listen."

She shook her head. "I'm sorry, Adam. But how did this one case screw things up for you? That seems a little harsh."

"That's how it goes in police work. I hadn't just screwed up a case. Another woman died because of me." His hand tightened on his beer bottle. "She died because I didn't find the real killer fast enough. I couldn't show my face at the station after that. I knew it was entirely because of my own stupid pride that I fucked everything up, but I also couldn't just quit being a cop. It's all I've ever wanted to be. With a record like mine, the only place that would take me is Huntsville, so here I am."

"I get that your pride caused tunnel vision, but it wasn't like you went out and killed someone. That's on the real murderer. Being exiled to Huntsville seems extreme."

He smiled sadly at her. "Huntsville isn't too bad. Not my favorite sheriff to work under though—I'll admit that."

She snorted into her drink. "Yeah, that's unsurprising, given that you have integrity, and Sheriff Holland is just a complete piece of shit."

Adam laughed. "Wow, tell me how you really feel."

She grinned at that. "You know I will."

"There's obviously some bad blood there—sort of like you have with everyone else in town," he added in a sarcastic tone, and she reached over and smacked his arm. "But what is it with Holland in particular?"

"I didn't think you'd need me to explain it to you

after he acted like such an asshole at the prayer meeting."

He shrugged. "He's always treated me like shit, though. He hates that I come from a big city. That I have more experience solving murders in just a few years on my old force than he's had in twenty years."

Just thinking of the way the sheriff acted earlier tonight made Erin's body tense. "He's an asshole to everyone. He shouldn't be working on Brooke and Steve's case—I'll put it that way. For one thing, I doubt he even cares that they're missing. He never has before."

Adam looked at her in that way of his, where she was sure he could see right through her to everything she was holding back. When she drained the rest of her drink, he raised an eyebrow at her. "Another?"

She shouldn't. Since Xanax was typically her drug of choice, she tended to not hold her alcohol. But she didn't want the night to end yet, so she got up and bought another round.

"Looks like I'm going to be walking you home," Adam said as he drank from his third beer.

"It's not a bad walk. It should take about the same amount of time it took me to get to the prayer meeting, and that was only a few minutes."

"I know I told you not to come, but I'm glad you did," he said. "I knew it would be tough for you to watch, though."

"Well, that makes one of us then. It took me by surprise," she said, alcohol loosening her tongue more than usual. "I didn't expect Janet to be that honest and heart-wrenching. She's like a completely different person." Horribly, her eyes teared up. "I realized as I listened to her describing Brooke that my baby sister isn't the person I remember either. I don't know anything about her, and it's entirely my fault. After what happened to me, all I cared about was leaving. I couldn't stay here another second, and I couldn't take Brooke with me. I convinced myself she'd be okay—at least until I got on my feet and could come get her."

Adam watched her with a gentle expression that made it even harder to swallow her tears. "Sounds reasonable to me. You were just a teenager, and you'd been through hell."

"I was the most responsible one in that house, though—trust me. Brooke needed me, and I just let the years go by. First I told myself I should finish college. And then I said I should finish up my internship. And then I needed to get my business off the ground. Before I knew it, thirteen years had gone by, and Brooke was almost grown up. I found out from my mother's speech that just looking at Brooke's Instagram every once in a while didn't tell me anything about who she is as a person."

"You came back when she needed you though."

She hung her head for a moment before meeting

his gaze. "Only because you convinced me to! The worst part was the guilt I struggled with for years over basically abandoning Brooke to be taken care of by an alcoholic prostitute—although I sent money and later set up a trust. I couldn't even bring myself to call her. I was terrified of what she'd say her life was like." She smiled at him through her tears. "So now you know I'm actually a horrible person."

He reached out and touched her arm, his hand warm. "You're not a horrible person. Janet pulled herself together and gave Brooke a great life. Brooke was her daughter—not yours."

"I know, but you don't understand how much I had to take care of Brooke growing up. She almost felt like mine."

"Do you have kids of your own?"

She shook her head. "I'm sure you'll be shocked to hear it, but I have serious trust issues. I've barely even had a relationship." She frowned. "I probably shouldn't be telling you all of this. You're the first man in a long time who hasn't made me feel like I'm trapped."

"It means a lot that you'd trust me," he said, holding her gaze for a beat. She couldn't look away from their coffee depths. "Especially after everything you've been through. I know it's been hell for you coming back here."

"It's been worse than I anticipated," she said, looking down at her drink. "But really, I shouldn't have been surprised by so many reacting to me that way. My family and I weren't well-loved when I lived here. Should give you plenty of suspects, though," she added with a wry smile.

His expression darkened. "It's been a long time, though. If they've forgiven Janet, I don't see why they haven't forgiven you." He took a sip of his beer contemplatively. "Maybe because you're the one who actually got out of this town."

"That could be. I know I'd be jealous of anyone who did if I was still trapped here."

He leaned forward, arms on the table. "Was there anyone you ever suspected of being the man who kidnapped you?"

"I don't know. It's something I've thought about so much, and maybe I would have figured it out if I stayed. Maybe I would have run into him in town and recognized his voice or...his smell." She shuddered as she thought of cigarettes and mildew. "For all I know, though, it could have been a complete stranger. I never saw his face."

His brows furrowed. "But at the time, he didn't seem familiar?"

"No. It was just a guy in the middle of the woods somewhere."

"And do you think it's this same guy who followed you to the gym and left you a message?"

She finished her drink and sat back against the seat.

She honestly hadn't even let herself entertain that idea. "I think it could be any of these assholes who don't want me back in this town. As you can see, they all treat me like the Boy Who Cried Wolf."

"I believe you," Adam said quietly.

She looked into his warm brown eyes and then down to his unexpectedly full lips. This was another reason she didn't drink: it made her want to kiss anyone with a pulse. And Adam just happened to be not only extremely hot, but also understanding and kind. Her heart picked up its pace.

"I'm tired," she said with an unsteady smile. "Ready to go?"

He stood and held out his hand to have her lead the way. "Sure. I'll walk you home."

With a few drinks in her, it was a lot harder to walk in heels. After she stumbled over a sidewalk crack for the second time, Adam pulled her close to his side and looped her arm through his. She sighed at the sudden support.

The alcohol dulled her anxiety that someone had been following her, but she was still glad Adam was with her. It brought a sense of peace she hadn't felt in a long time.

At this time of night, there weren't many cars out. It was mostly quiet, and Adam clearly didn't feel the need to break the silence with endless prattle.

Before she knew it, they arrived at her ugly motel.

She fumbled for her keys for a moment, and then turned to thank him. Once again, their gazes caught. She didn't even think about it. She stepped into his broad chest, reached a hand up to his rough cheek, and pressed her lips to his.

He stiffened in shock for a breath, but then his arms were strong around her, and his mouth opened against hers. Their tongues mingled, the taste of alcohol still fresh.

Erin reveled in the feel of his strong arms around her, at the contrast of her soft breasts meeting a rock-hard chest. For the first time in a long time, she didn't feel disgusted or afraid. She only wanted more. When they came up for a breath, Erin said, "Do you want to come inside?"

Adam didn't immediately let go of her, and he took a shuddering breath. "I want to, but I shouldn't. It wouldn't be right. Not now. Not tonight."

She could feel his arousal, so she knew it wasn't a total rejection. She also knew that she could easily seduce him and push him over the edge into coming into her room. But her pride wouldn't let her.

"I'll see you tomorrow then," she said, pulling away from him and opening the door at the same time.

"Erin, I—"

But she shut the door in his face and didn't hear whatever he was about to say.

She stumbled through her room, pulling off clothes

at random before heading into her bathroom to pee. That done, she pulled back the covers and practically fell into bed.

A sense of wrongness enveloped her the moment her head touched the pillow. The pleasant, woozy sensation of too much drink drained away almost instantly. She lay there, heart pounding. What was it?

The faintest scent of cigarettes reached her nose, and she sat up in a rush. Had she imagined it? She pulled back the covers more and discovered that the sheets were rumpled, even though the maid service had already been in to clean up.

As she reached to run her hand over the wrinkled sheets, she jerked it back with a yelp. The bed was warm, like someone had just been lying in it.

17

THEN

Erin's feet ached from working a double shift with no breaks, but she desperately needed the money. Janet had screwed up again and now they owed the landlord for last month's rent. He swore up and down this time he'd evict them, and then where would they go? Erin and Brooke had no father to run to, no family of any kind, really. They'd be on the streets in no time. Or lost in the foster system.

She hated to do double shifts not only because they were brutal, especially after a full day at school, but because she had to leave Brooke at home under the dubious care of their mother. It was just too long to expect a four-year-old to behave at a diner, so Erin didn't really have a choice.

There were only about ten minutes left in her shift, but she had to wait until the last of her customers were finished so she could collect the max amount of tips. She plastered a smile on her face and went around from table to table, refilling drinks or bringing checks. They dwindled away slowly, and she tried not to glance at the clock too often, but it was hard not to.

"Hurry up, dammit," she hissed under her breath as she watched the last customer finish the last of his meal with agonizing slowness.

Midnight had come and gone, but she wanted to wait for the pathetic two-dollar tip he was sure to leave her.

At last, he lumbered away from the table, and she rushed over, not even bothering to wait to make sure he wasn't watching her snatch up the cash. She stopped short when she saw the two quarters waiting by his plate.

"Son of a bitch," she said, anger momentarily giving her a burst of energy as she snapped her gaze to his back.

He gave a little wave to Eddie and left, completely without shame that he'd left such a shitty tip to a girl having to pay her family's rent.

After pulling out her tips, she stomped back behind the counter and ripped off her apron. She made the mistake of catching Eddie's eye, and she groaned under her breath when he came over.

"Bad night, honey?" he asked, and she bristled all over.

"I'm just tired. I'll see you later, Eddie."

He blocked her way around the counter with a hairy arm. "Want a ride home?"

Her eyes flashed. "I thought you said you'd never give me a ride home again."

He gave her a lazy grin. "You know I was just mad that night."

"I can make it on my own."

She slipped past his arm and grabbed her bag. Before she could turn around again, he came up behind her. He was so close, she could smell his sickening cologne. "It's pretty dangerous to walk home at night. A young girl like you. You'd be safe with me."

She scoffed and maneuvered so she was facing him again. "First of all, this is Huntsville. Nothing ever happens here. And second of all, I'm not going anywhere with you."

His face darkened. "You'd think with a whore for a mom, you'd be a lot easier."

All of Erin's emotions of disgust, exhaustion, and anger came to a boil, and she struck out. She hit him so hard across the cheek it snapped his head to the side. Her palm stung.

Clutching his cheek, he growled out, "You can consider yourself fired for that, you bitch."

"Yeah, well, I quit."

She turned on her heel and stormed out of the diner, adrenaline from the slap at least making her forget about her aching feet and utter exhaustion for a few minutes.

But soon, as the moon glowed softly above her, and the crickets and frogs made their nightly serenade, her limbs grew heavy. She followed the road, staying on the gravelly shoulder. Beyond her were the woods, though she tried not to think too hard about that. She'd never seen so much as a deer on her walks home, but it still made her nervous to think something could be there watching her and she'd never know it.

She tried to turn her thoughts to happier things, like falling into bed and curling up with Brooke. That only made her start to worry about whether Brooke had eaten a decent dinner and if Janet had even bothered to put her to bed on time.

She almost didn't hear the car until it was right up next to her. It was unusual enough that there was a car out this late, and her first thought was that Eddie had come after her. She whirled around to lay into him, only to realize it wasn't Eddie's car at all. It was a loud, diesel-engine truck, and it pulled over just behind her. The hair on the back of her neck stood up. She picked up her pace.

The driver's door squeaked open, and the sound of boots hitting gravel made her whimper in fear. She dared to turn around for just a moment, only to see it was a man wearing a black ski mask. Her legs nearly gave out. She couldn't think of many reasons someone would be wearing a ski mask at night, but none of them were good.

Erin took off at a sprint for the woods. The pounding of footsteps behind her rang out in the quiet night. Her breaths came in a panicked rush, and she tried to zigzag around trees.

He overtook her easily. She was young and strong, but also exhausted from school and work, and he'd gotten the jump on her. Still, she fought him like a wild animal, thrashing and clawing and kicking.

His arms were like iron bands around her. And then he held a rough piece of cloth over her nose and mouth. She gasped and gagged, but then her eyes closed against her will. She couldn't fight it, couldn't even will her limbs to fight back.

The word flitted through her mind, then. The word that explained what was happening to her.

Kidnapped.

He was kidnapping her.

And then everything went black.

18

NOW

Erin sat back on her heels and grabbed a wad of toilet paper to press against her mouth. After flushing down the vomit, she stood shakily. As she rinsed her mouth out at the sink, her watering eyes led to tears of self-pity. She didn't know if she suffered from a hangover from drinking so much last night, or if the panic-inducing discovery that someone had been in her bed had finally broken her.

She stumbled back to the rock-hard chair she'd slept in last night and sat down. With her legs tucked up close to her chest, she wrapped her arms around them. The moment when she discovered the wrinkled sheets and the warm spot in her bed raced through her mind again. The implications covered her body in goosebumps. Someone had been watching her, first at the gym and now here. More disturbingly: someone had been in her room. In her *bed*.

It was like a fucked-up version of *Goldilocks and the Three Bears*. Only this one gave you nightmares.

She may have been drunk last night, but she wasn't drunk at the gym when her panties were stolen and there was a message on the mirror. And she knew someone had been lying in her bed—there was no other explanation for that one spot to be so warm.

She rested her pounding head on her legs and glanced at her phone. Seven a.m. No missed calls.

At her weakest moment last night, when she thought she might start screaming and never stop, she'd briefly considered calling Adam. After his rejection, though, her pride wouldn't let her. Would he have even believed her? He had so far, but this time, she was undeniably drunk. He could have easily chalked it up to that, and the thought of him telling her she must be suffering from drunken paranoia made her weep. Or worse, he might have even thought she was trying to manipulate him into her bed. Both scenarios had caused her to put down the phone and spend the night with her eyes wide open.

In between moments where she seriously considered going to the ER for heart palpitations, she'd racked her brain over who could be responsible.

Who was sick enough to do something like that? Preacher Bob came to mind. He had been a complete asshole from the second he saw her. The sheriff, too, had been outwardly aggressive to her. He probably even had connections to be able to sneak into her room. Had he wanted to send her a message so she'd leave town? Did he hate her that much?

Of course, Sheriff Holland wasn't the only one who wouldn't be happy she was back in town. She tried never to think about his son, not after everything that had happened between them. On the rare chances she did, she wondered what had happened to him. If there was justice in the world, he had hopefully been castrated. She never wanted to see him again, but if it helped Brooke, she'd do it. She hadn't heard a whisper about him since she got here, and she didn't know if he even lived here anymore. But maybe it was time to find out.

Coffee might help her feel better, but she couldn't stand the weak stuff the hotel served. The thought of getting up and going out made her stomach reel. Still, it would only make her anxiety reach cataclysmic levels if she stayed cooped up in this hotel room.

With Adam likely enduring a tirade from Sheriff Holland this morning, she wouldn't have a free ride. She'd just have to do a little snooping on her own. This wasn't a town with taxis at every street corner, so it was a good thing she didn't mind walking.

After popping some aspirin and downing a whole bottle of water, Erin got dressed for the day. She wore the only pair of jeans she brought and a flowy black blouse because she honestly couldn't even contemplate wearing heels today. Flats were the way to go.

As she applied mascara in the mirror, a horrible thought flitted across her mind. What if it was *him*? What if he was stalking her now that she'd come back?

Nausea rose fast and hard within her, and she had to run water on the inside of her wrists to keep from puking again. She mentally shook herself and pushed away those thoughts. For her own sanity, she couldn't entertain them.

Her phone rang, and she looked at the screen eagerly, hoping it was Adam. When she saw Nikki's name instead, she groaned. By her mostly-cleared out inbox, she knew that Nikki was handling things beautifully while she was gone. If she was calling again, it was because Christopher Roland was stirring up trouble.

"Hi, Nikki," Erin said, forcing herself not to sound too miserable.

"Erin, I'm so sorry. It's Christopher Roland again. He's desperate to speak with you—I think you being gone has just really thrown him for a loop. He's been… needier than usual."

Erin snorted into the phone. "Shocking. Okay, put

him through, and I'll see if I can talk him off the ledge."

"Erin," his voice boomed into the speaker in a rush, "my God, I've been dying to speak with you. Wasting away. Nikki is fabulous—you know that. But there's just no substitute for you. Only you can handle something this horrible, this soul-crushing."

"I'm so sorry, Christopher. I had an urgent family matter to take care of, and I haven't returned to the office yet, but I still have time to talk. What's going on?"

"Nikki just sent over the materials for the newest ad campaign—you know, the one that features my most breathtaking designs. The moment I saw it, I fell out of my chair. I literally fell down—I think I must have fainted. It was that bad, Erin. It was *that* bad. I screamed so loud I scared my poor fur baby, Tybalt."

"That's terrible news, Christopher. And I can assure you I will do everything I can to fix this for you. What didn't you like about the ad campaign?"

"Have you seen it? You have to look at it. You'll know as soon as you do. You'll be horrified—I know it. Go ahead, pull it up. I'll wait."

Erin stifled a sigh. She had seen the ad campaign, of course. She'd overseen the creation of it, after all. All that was left before she flew down to West Virginia was the finalization of a few design elements, ones that her team were more than capable of handling. She was confident the campaign was flashy, cutting-edge, and fashion-forward.

"Okay, I have it pulled up, Christopher."

"So you see it? It's hideous. It honestly hurts my eyes to look at it."

"Why don't you just tell me what you're seeing so I know we're on the same page."

"The font! It's like Comic Sans. It's *worse* than Comic Sans. It's huge and loopy and childlike—not edgy and fashionable at all. I'll be the laughingstock of the fashion world."

Erin knew it would be something small and nit-picky like this, and she was prepared. "Christopher, I completely agree with you. I'm going to have design change it right away. I'm emailing them as we speak."

There was nothing wrong with the font, she knew, but it was far easier to change that and make Christopher happy than to fight with him and insist on keeping something they didn't need.

He let out an explosive breath. "Oh Erin, you beautiful creature. Oh, this makes me feel so much better. Like I can breathe again."

"You're so welcome, Christopher. I'll have them send you a list of font choices so you can give your approval, okay?"

"That is the perfect solution! I knew you'd know what to do. Thank you so much, Erin. What an absolute relief."

"Of course, and I'm so happy I could help you. Now, I have a car waiting on me, so I'm going to have to let you go."

"Ciao, darling," he said.

Relieved he let her off the hook so easily, Erin gathered up her things and sent a quick email to Nikki to let her know how it went.

Erin went by the hotel lobby before stepping out. When the receptionist at the front desk saw her, she waved her over.

"Ms. Masters? A gentleman left these for you this morning and said he wanted to be sure you got them."

She handed Erin a box of chocolates wrapped in a red bow. Erin looked for a note, but there was none. As she'd never received chocolates from anyone in her life, she looked at it in utter confusion for a few moments. The only person she knew here was Adam, and with a sinking feeling, she remembered last night. With a groan, she rubbed her face. She couldn't believe she kissed him like that. She hoped he hadn't taken any of that the wrong way—she just got super flirty when she was drunk. It was why she usually stuck to pills. She couldn't stand to act like Janet. Nothing serious was ever going to happen between them anyway—when this was over, she was going back to her life in New York.

She just hoped he understood that, too.

E rin walked for about a block to the only cafe in town. Freshly roasted coffee beans and a yeasty-sweet smell of pastry enveloped her the moment she walked in, and she let out a breath in relief when her stomach growled instead of churning with nausea. After ordering an Americano, she settled in with her phone. The barista here looked too young to know anything about Norma, so she'd have to use social media to snoop.

It didn't take long to find her. There were only two Normas in Huntsville, and Erin would recognize that same hideous 1990s haircut anywhere. Her profile wasn't even set to private. She didn't provide details of where she worked, but a quick scroll through her photos gave Erin all the information she needed. There were pictures of Norma wearing an apron at the local grocery store, so Erin figured that would be a good place to start searching for her.

She finished her Americano, and then went back and ordered another one to go, because she still felt like shit. The café was located in the middle of town, so she could just walk the few blocks to the grocery store.

Piggly Wiggly had always been the biggest store in town, and nothing much had changed since Erin lived there. The old-fashioned sign with a Porky Pig-looking character hung above a large brick grocery store with a packed parking lot.

Inside was surprisingly busy, with most of the lanes full of waiting shoppers. Erin spotted her on the third register from the end, but she wasn't prepared for the visceral reaction she experienced. The coffee burned like acid in her stomach, and her whole body drew taut as a bow. All she could think about was the last time she saw Norma, in the women's bathroom at church.

She opened one of the soft drink coolers, grabbed two bottles of water, and joined the line for Norma's register. Norma robotically scanned groceries and never once looked toward the end of the line where Erin waited, so she had a chance to observe her. Her frizzy hair had streaks of gray and bags hung under her eyes. She barely said anything to the customers at checkout beyond a grudging hello and their price total. Her obvious misery was a soothing balm to Erin's heart.

Finally, Norma scanned Erin's two bottles of water. It took her a moment to glance up at Erin, but when she did, all the color left her face, and her eyes widened.

"Hello, Norma," Erin said with a mean smile. "We need to talk."

"I don't have anything to say to you," Norma said with a furtive glance at the old lady slowly unloading her cartful of groceries behind Erin.

Erin shrugged. "I'll be happy to say what I need to right here—in front of everyone—or we can go someplace quiet and talk. It's your call."

She huffed out her breath. "Fine. I'll take my break after this next customer. You can just wait over there." She nodded her head toward the doors, and Erin paid her for the water.

Norma turned off the number above her register and placed a "Lane Closed" sign at the end of the old lady's groceries. She did this with frequent glares at Erin, as if she hoped she could intimidate her into giving up and leaving. As if it was that easy.

After helping the old lady run her check through several times, Norma finally left her register and walked toward Erin. She looked like someone sentenced to death. Her wrinkled face had a gray cast to it.

"Back here," Norma said and led Erin to the loading dock, which was clearly a favorite smoke break spot if all the cigarette butts were any indication.

The sun burned overhead as Norma squinted her eyes at Erin. "What do you want?"

"I want to know where Rick is."

Norma folded her arms across her chest. "How the hell should I know? You see this name tag on my chest? It doesn't say Holland anymore."

"You have kids together. You must know something." Rick was a creep and a predator. He took complete advantage of Erin when she was just a girl. If someone took Brooke, then Erin had to consider everyone a suspect, and Rick was one person she knew for sure who liked young girls.

"I divorced that bastard years ago, and he left town ten years back. He didn't care about his kids. They haven't heard from him since he left, same as me. You shouldn't have bothered me at work. If anyone knows where he is, it's his father."

"Somehow I don't think Sheriff Holland will be as forthcoming with information about Rick."

Norma sneered at her. "You know, I'm surprised you didn't keep in touch with him. You two were so in love, right? Disgusting."

"It was disgusting—on his part. He's a manipulative pedophile, and you were the one married to him."

Norma pursed her lips. "I'm guessing you're back in town because of Brooke. I don't understand why everyone is panicking and running around looking for that girl and her simple-minded boyfriend. Teenagers run away all the time and act stupid."

Erin had thought the same thing once, but she hated hearing it from Norma's mouth. "You never did care about other kids, did you Norma? You were willing to blame a seventeen-year-old for something your perverted husband did. You even accosted me in the church bathroom. Some Christian you are."

Norma narrowed her eyes. "Like you're some innocent angel. I can tell you where your sister went. She's probably off being a slut with her boyfriend, just like you, and just like your mother."

Rage bubbled up inside Erin so fast she nearly choked on it. She lashed out with her hand, slapping Norma hard across the face. She caught the side of the older woman's nose, and it started to bleed.

"My nose!" Norma shouted, catching the blood in her hand.

Erin didn't experience even a second of remorse. "I've waited thirteen years to do that."

She walked away, leaving Norma crying and bleeding on the loading dock.

19

In the parking lot of the Piggly Wiggly, Erin stood beneath the shade of a skinny tree and tried to figure out what to do next. As satisfying as it was to have finally given Norma what she deserved, the fact that Rick seemed to be a dead end made Erin want to go a few rounds with a punching bag. She knew she would have gotten sick satisfaction if it turned out the sheriff's son was behind all this, but the fact that his ex-wife had no idea where he was seemed problematic. Was he fooling everyone and just hiding out in that horrible cabin in the woods? And if so, where was he going for supplies?

She shook her head. It might not be a complete dead end, but it was beyond her dubious sleuthing abilities. She'd have to tell Adam about him and see if he could dig up anything more worthwhile.

If it wasn't Rick, then who could it be?

Erin thought of others in her town, men who might know both her and Brooke. As she cast her thoughts back to her childhood here, her time at Eddie's Diner popped into her head. Not only was Eddie clearly a creep, but he knew them both. Working through the town's unsettling list of pedophiles seemed a logical way to investigate.

The restaurant was still in business, so was Eddie still working there?

Only one way to find out.

Nostalgia hit Erin hard as she traced the same route she used to take to the diner. She remembered how it used to take forever to walk the few blocks because she usually had Brooke in tow. Her little legs hadn't been able to keep up, and Erin always ended up having to carry her.

A chime from her phone interrupted her reverie. She glanced at it to see a text from Adam.

I've been at the station all morning, so I'm sorry I couldn't pick you up. Want to grab some lunch?

Erin texted back that she was walking to Eddie's Diner and to meet her there. Might as well kill two birds with one stone.

As she walked, she thought about the chocolates again but decided against mentioning them. It was probably better to feel him out first and see if he was extra attentive. She grimaced. She hoped she wouldn't have to deal with a situation like that on top of everything else. The last thing she needed now was to navigate someone's amorous feelings. She just wanted to find out what happened to Brooke. That was the priority. Everything else was a distraction.

When she saw the diner, Erin tried to stop the onslaught of memories. All the times she came here with little Brooke or worked until her feet hurt worse than stomping around New York City in high heels. From the outside, it looked exactly the same.

Inside, though, had been renovated a bit. It was meant to look like a vintage diner with red faux leather booths, posters of movie stars from the fifties, and black and white checkered flooring. It at least appeared cleaner than when she'd worked there. After a quick glance around, she saw Adam wasn't there yet.

Taking a booth in one of the back corners that Brooke used to nap in, Erin waited for one of the waitresses to notice her. Finally, a girl came over who was not much older than Erin had been when she worked there, her eyes heavily lined and her hair dyed black.

She smiled at Erin. "What can I get you?"

"I'll just have water for now, but can I ask you something?"

The girl nodded, looking wary.

"Is Eddie, the owner, here today? Can I speak with him?"

The girl shot her a sympathetic look. "Oh, I hate to

tell you this, but Eddie died four years ago. It was before I started working here, so I never met him."

Erin's hopes plummeted. "Wow, okay. Thanks for letting me know."

"Sure thing. Let me get that water for you."

Erin looked down at the table when she walked away, trying to process what she said. So now two of her leads had turned out to be complete dead ends. Failure of this magnitude was unfamiliar to Erin, and it made her feel completely incompetent.

Maybe her first instinct about the situation with Brooke was correct. Maybe she really had just run off with Steve. Erin would absolutely hate for Norma to be right about that, but it was the one thing that made Brooke's case different from her own disappearance. Or even the disappearance of the other girls Adam had learned about. At the same time, though, she desperately wanted it to be true that Brooke had run away. The alternatives filled her with a sense of cold dread.

She thought about all the emails and PR business she'd been neglecting, and pulled up a list of available flights on her phone. Clearly she wasn't helping anyone by being here. Not only that, but hell if she was going to subject herself to more mind games from whomever it was leaving her vaguely threatening messages.

By the time Adam joined her, she'd already booked a flight back to New York for later that day.

"I hope you already ordered," Adam said with a nod at her glass of water. "You didn't have to wait on me."

"I don't know if I can eat now, honestly—not after striking out twice today before noon."

"What do you mean?"

She took a sip of water and leaned back in the booth, suddenly tired. The coffee from earlier must have worn off. "I thought I was so clever by tracking down the two men who used to sexually harass me when I was Brooke's age. One was my English teacher Rick Holland, Sheriff Holland's son."

Adam's eyebrows lifted. "Now that's some dirt I didn't know."

"Yeah, but his ex-wife said he's been gone for ten years. She doesn't even know where he is anymore. And the other guy was the owner of this diner, Eddie. He was my sleazy boss when I worked here back in the day, but apparently he's been dead for four years."

"Well, damn," he said with a shake of his head. "Those were good choices for suspects, especially since you have a personal history with them. That's exactly what I wanted you to come here to help with."

"All I've managed to do since I got here is piss people off and solve exactly nothing. I'm no closer to figuring out what happened to Brooke than I was a few days ago. Also the fact that both she and her boyfriend are missing has always been suspicious. It just doesn't add up because it's not like all the other kidnapping cases."

"I hear you, but I still think they're related somehow. I can feel it in my gut."

Erin gave him a knowing look. "Your gut has been wrong before."

Adam leaned back like she'd smacked him, hurt flashing across his face just for a moment. Erin felt like shit—she shouldn't have used what he'd told her last night against him. But then the waitress came and interrupted them, so she had to sit there and stew on her bad behavior while he ordered.

"I'm sorry, Adam," Erin said with a sigh when the waitress left. "I shouldn't have said that. You trusted me with your past, and I don't mean to throw it back in your face." Before he could respond, she added, "While I'm apologizing, I should also add that I'm sorry for throwing myself on you like that last night and propositioning you."

He put down his glass and met her gaze. "I'm not." When her eyes widened, he said, a little loudly. "The kiss—I meant the kiss. I don't regret that. I didn't like turning you down, but you seemed like you'd had a little too much whiskey. I didn't want you waking up and, rightly, thinking I took advantage of you if I accepted your offer."

Erin's face warmed. "I get extra clingy and flirty

when I drink—it's why I don't usually drink that much."

Adam grinned. "I liked talking to you, though. It's been a long time since I had someone to listen to my bullshit for hours."

"Me too," Erin said, but then she sighed. "Shared bullshitting aside, all I've done here is stir the pot and distract you from doing what you need to do to find Brooke and Steve. That's why I'm flying back to New York today. I'm clearly not cut out for police work, so I need to get back to what I *am* good at."

His expression turned serious. "I get that you're frustrated, but I don't think you should leave yet. I didn't know about your connection with Rick Holland or Eddie, for one thing. Those are great leads."

She shook her head. "Except that they're both completely out of the picture and have been for years."

"Yeah, but potential suspects aren't the only thing you can help me with." He took a deep breath and held her gaze. "The main reason I asked you to come back to Huntsville is to retrace your steps from the night you escaped."

Erin blanched. She shouldn't have been surprised —it made sense, after all. It had been all she'd ever wanted when she was a teenager. She'd imagined the police following her through the woods, bloodhounds in the lead, and catching the monster who took her.

But Sheriff Holland had dashed those hopes the moment she stepped foot in the police station all those years ago.

She rubbed her arms as sweat broke out over her body. "I don't know if I can."

Adam reached out and took her hand. "I know it'll be hard for you, but I want you to think of Brooke. What if it helps us find her?"

She closed her eyes. She knew he had a point. "All right."

"Will you cancel your flight? If we don't find anything, then I'll drive you to the airport tomorrow myself."

With a sigh, she took out her phone and cancelled the flight, eating the cancellation fee. She hated to waste money like that, but she'd do anything to help Brooke.

Even if it meant going back into those nightmare woods.

After Adam had wolfed down a cheeseburger, fries, a chocolate milkshake, and then convinced Erin to at least eat a plate of scrambled eggs and toast, he drove them to the approximate area where Erin had been taken.

It hadn't been far from the diner, maybe half a mile or so. And the woods bordered the main road into town, so she hadn't been far from help. But of course, it never came.

Now that she stood on the shoulder of the same road she'd been abducted on, her legs shook, her stomach threatened to throw up the eggs, and her headache returned with a fierce vengeance. She thought of the moment the truck had appeared behind her. Of the sound of his footsteps…the rough feel of the cloth over her face. Suddenly, it was like she'd been plunged underwater. She couldn't breathe. She was starved for air, and her lungs refused to function.

A warm, gentle hand touched her arm. "Just breathe," Adam said quietly. Her gaze darted to his. "That's it. One breath at a time." He took deep breaths too, slowly in and out, and she found she started to unconsciously imitate him.

The flood of oxygen eased some of the pressure in her chest.

"You're safe now, okay?" Adam said, holding her gaze with his big eyes.

She watched him for a moment and just concentrated on breathing. Finally, she felt steady enough to go on.

"Tell me something so I don't think about it all," she said. "What did the sheriff say to you?"

"He just busted my balls for thirty minutes, saying I never should have contacted you about all this. I told him that was bullshit since it's your sister who's missing. Felt good to smart off like that, but of course it only pissed him off more."

They headed into the woods, stepping carefully over logs and underbrush, and Erin was glad she'd worn flats for once.

"I'm sorry I was the cause of you getting talked down to by that lunatic."

Adam shrugged. "He threatened to fire me if I continue with my so-called conspiracy theories of multiple girls being taken across states, but it's obvious what he's really mad about."

He held a branch aside for her as she sent him a questioning glance. "And what's that?"

"If it turns out Brooke's disappearance is connected to the other girls and yours, then that means he didn't do his damn job thirteen years ago," Adam said with a sharp tone she hadn't heard him take before. "He dismissed you as a lying teenager when you were a victim, and now he's brought this evil down on the town again."

Erin hadn't thought of it that way, but it rang true. That wasn't the only reason the sheriff hated her though. He hated her for getting Rick fired—not because he cared about his son, really. He just cared about how the whole pedo situation reflected on him as sheriff. Evidently, no one gave a shit because he was still sheriff of this town. Funny how both of them had abused their power while in positions of authority. The apple didn't fall far from the tree with Rick and his dad.

"I'm glad you believe me," Erin said, and he glanced back at her.

"I'm sorry no one else did when it counted most."

She tried to pretend that didn't make her eyes sting with tears.

"You've definitely made this town bearable," she said. "Last night was…fun."

He grinned. "I mean, *I* thought so, but then I figured you'd just chalk it up to too much whiskey."

"Well, that was a lot of whiskey for me, but I still enjoyed spending time with you. Thanks for the chocolates, too, by the way."

He was quiet for a moment, and she glanced back to see his face looked puzzled. "Chocolates? What do you mean?"

Before Erin could respond, she tripped over something and fell down hard.

Expecting another fallen log, it took her brain a moment to process what she was seeing. She noticed the swarm of black flies first. And then the smell enveloped her: a sickly, putrid rotting. When she looked down to see what the flies were swarming around, she screamed.

It was a body, bloated and badly deteriorated from being scavenged by animals and other forest creatures. While she gagged and scuttled away, Adam checked the clothing for identification.

"Shit," Adam said, his expression full of dismay. "It's Steve."

20

THEN

E rin asked the driver of the truck, an older man with a graying beard, to drive her straight to the police station. He took one look at her and did as she asked. The whole way there, all she could think about was that justice was about to be served. The monster who held her for days against her will, who tortured her in ways she hadn't imagined possible, would be hunted down like an animal and locked up forever. He'd never be able to do this to another girl again.

When her Good Samaritan driver pulled in front

of the station, he turned to her as she opened her door, "Do you want me to go in with you?"

Erin shook her head. "You've done enough for me. Thank you for saving me back there."

This was the first of his questions she'd actually answered. He'd tried to get her to tell him what happened to her, but she couldn't find the words. She'd saved them all up for the police and had no more to spare.

"Thank you," she whispered again and shut the door before he could say anything else.

He watched her head into the police station, and then she heard his truck drive away.

In the harsh fluorescent lights, she knew she looked like an absolute wreck. Her face, hands, and legs were streaked with blood from various cuts and scratches she'd acquired in her flight through the woods. There were leaves and twigs stuck in her hair and clothes. Her clothing was filthy and raggedy, and she was barefoot.

As the night receptionist ran over to her side, asking her questions, the shock of everything hit her at once. She shook uncontrollably and had to wrap her arms around herself just to keep from falling apart.

At some point, the receptionist convinced her to follow her to the sheriff's office, and with a promise to fetch her some hot chocolate, she left her alone with Sheriff Holland.

He watched her from behind his large desk dispassionately. His small eyes were narrowed, like she stood before him as a criminal instead of a shaking girl.

"What brings you in this late at night?" he asked, like it was some kind of casual visit. For a moment, she was stunned into silence. Didn't he know she'd been missing for a week?

"I'm here to report a kidnapping."

He steepled his hands in front of him and lifted his eyebrows. "Yeah? Whose?"

"My own! I've been missing for a week!"

"Funny, I don't have any report of you being missing."

Erin shook harder. Her own mother hadn't even noticed she was gone? "I walked home from working at Eddie's Monday night, and a guy in a diesel pickup pulled up behind me. He was wearing a black ski mask. When he started chasing after me, I tried to run into the woods, but he caught me." Her voice broke, and she hugged herself tightly.

"He held something against my mouth, and it made me pass out. When I came to, I was in a basement. That's where he…" she trailed off, unable to finish. The horrors of the last week took hold of her, and for several terrible seconds, it felt like she was still there. Still trapped in that dark, dank basement with him.

"He tortured me," she forced herself to say. "In every way a girl can be tortured. I thought I would die, and sometimes I prayed for death. But every day I worked on my escape. He didn't think I could fit through that window or that I could get it unstuck. And he never left his house, but finally, one night, I heard him start up his truck and go."

"I ran through the woods, just looking for the road. I figured if I could make it there, I could flag someone down. And that's exactly what I did. The driver brought me straight here."

She expected a flurry of questions from the sheriff. He'd listened without comment, his expression cold and unfeeling. He didn't even ask her to sit down. Erin's body stung and ached in every muscle, but if he said he needed her to show him the way right now, she would go. Anything to lock up her kidnapper.

The sheriff leaned forward, his heavy stomach nearly resting on his desk. "Well now that's quite the story, Ms. Lewis. And maybe if you hadn't made up that horrible lie about my son, who lost his job and had his career destroyed all because you came onto him in his own classroom, then maybe I'd believe you. But unfortunately, Ms. Lewis, I think you're an attention-seeking liar."

Erin's eyes filled with tears. She didn't know what to say, how to react. Never in her wildest dreams had she imagined going to the cops and the cops not caring. Not listening to her. And this was the sheriff!

"Will you go looking for the man who took me?"

In answer, the sheriff leaned back in his chair and put his feet up on his desk. "Oh yeah. I'll get right on it." She flinched, and his eyes narrowed again. "Now go on home and get out of my face."

Erin turned on her heel and nearly ran into the receptionist. The woman's eyes widened as she held a steaming cup of hot chocolate in her hand. A loud sob escaped Erin as she fled from the room. She couldn't bear to hear Sheriff Holland tell the kind woman that Erin was a liar.

She ran all the way home.

21

THEN

E rin stood in front of her house, shaking and pouring sweat. She'd pushed her broken body too hard by running home, even though it was only a few blocks from the police station —just in the bad part of town. But panic had nipped at her heels like wolves. With the sheriff against her, she felt like her kidnapper might appear at any moment, and no one would lift a finger to help her.

She hurried up the dilapidated porch steps and pulled open the broken screen door. She closed the front door tightly after she entered the house and forced the flimsy lock closed. Her house had never seemed so vulnerable to a break-in.

No one waited to greet her when she walked in and something inside Erin deflated. She limped into the living room and found a complete wreck: old food, plates, cups, trash, and toys strewn about everywhere. In their tiny kitchen, a layer of filth covered the floor, the sink overflowed with dirty dishes, and she couldn't even see the counters anymore because they were completely covered with food and trash.

The cuts on the bottom of her feet stung with every step down the hall. Tears flowed unchecked down her cheeks, and in her mind, she kept repeating, *Mama.* She couldn't remember a time she'd wanted her mother to hold her, but she'd never been more desperate for it now. Just outside her mother's room, the sounds of the TV flowed out into the hall.

"Mama," Erin said, her voice breaking.

Her mother lounged on the bed with a forty in her hand, but jerked upright at the sound of her name.

"Hey!" she yelled, her voice slurring terribly. "The school called 'cause you didn't show up! You better give me a piece of all that money you been making at the diner if I'm gonna cover for your ass!"

Erin stood for a moment, just staring at the train wreck that was her mother. She knew she shouldn't have expected a better reception, especially after what happened with the sheriff. But still. Frustration and hurt climbed up her throat, and she knew she'd start screaming like a crazy person if she stayed there for another second.

A sob escaped as she continued to her room, stumbling with fatigue. Inside their room, Brooke sat in front of the TV, eyes glazed over. Erin's gaze swept over her little sister's dirty clothes and tangled hair, her fists tightening at the obvious neglect. When Brooke caught sight of Erin, she immediately jumped to her feet.

"Erin!" she cried out in her sweet Minnie Mouse voice as she launched herself at Erin's midsection. Erin winced as she made contact with her various injuries, but she wrapped her arms tightly around her sister anyway. "Where were you? What happened?"

"I was just lost in the woods for a while, baby," Erin said, her voice hitching as she held her sister close. "I'm fine now."

"I missed you so much, Erin," she said, rubbing her little face on Erin's stomach.

Erin tried to hold back tears. She didn't want to break down in front of Brooke and scare her little sister. "I missed you, too. Hey, are you hungry?" When Brooke nodded emphatically, Erin added, "Let's go get you something to eat, okay?"

They padded down the hall and into the filthy kitchen. Erin pulled out a half-eaten box of Pop-Tarts and put a couple into the toaster. She checked the fridge for some milk, but there was nothing on the shelves except for a couple of eggs and beer. She filled up a little cup of water for her instead and gave her the toaster pastries on a paper towel.

"I'm going to take a shower while you eat those," Erin said, leading her sister back to their room. When she passed their mother's room, she saw that she'd passed out on the bed. Disgust warred with relief inside her. At least she wouldn't have to deal with more of her bullshit on top of everything else tonight.

Their bathroom miraculously wasn't too dirty, probably because their mother hadn't given Brooke a bath since Erin wasn't there to do it for her. Erin turned the water on as hot as she could stand and stepped in. The tub drain had never worked well, and water pooled around her feet, making her cuts sting. Blood and dirt tinged the water brown, and she couldn't bear to look at it. She hissed as the shower spray hit her open wounds, but she took a piece of soap and a washcloth and scrubbed every inch of herself so hard she turned pink all over. Her tears mingled with the water, and no matter how hard she washed, she still felt dirty.

After drying off with a towel that smelled less than fresh, she put on a t-shirt and comfortable shorts and fell into bed beside Brooke. She had already fallen asleep, and Erin curled herself around her sister. Brooke sleepily patted Erin's arm. "It's okay, Erin," she mumbled.

Erin lowered her head into her sister's hair and broke down in tears.

22

NOW

L ike an ant hill that had been kicked, the small police station buzzed with activity. Ever since their horrible discovery of Steve's body, cops were constantly moving from the station to the crime scene and back again. Erin waited for Adam to return in his cramped cubicle space, her mind reliving the moment she stumbled over poor Steve. They'd driven straight to the station, so she still wore the clothes she'd had on. Mud streaked her pants, but thankfully the body hadn't been covered in blood.

Steve's death changed everything. It opened terrifying questions that shook Erin to her core, no longer able to cling to the idea that the young lovers had run off together. Where was Brooke? Was she dead, too? Every time Erin thought of that possibility, her throat closed up. The only thing that kept her going was the idea that if they were both killed, surely Brooke's body would've been there with Steve's. Adam said that by the decomposition of the body, it had been there a while. Possibly since the day they went missing.

Adam returned with a steaming cup of stale coffee. It tasted as bad as it smelled, but it was hot, and Erin took it gratefully.

"The sheriff is off breaking the news to Steve's parents," he said, sitting down on his chair. His gaze met hers. "Are you doing okay?"

Erin's eyes filled with tears. "I think you may have been right about everything…about Brooke being taken just like I was. I think a big part of why I came down here was to prove to myself and to you that she'd just run off with Steve in some show of teenage rebellion, but now he's—" she cut herself off before she started crying in earnest. All she could see was Steve's bloated face. The animals and insects in the forest had not been kind, and she knew she'd never get that image of him out of her head.

Adam leaned over and hugged her, his strong arms wrapping around her tightly. She melted into his warmth. "I'm sorry you had to find out that way," he said. "I don't want you to give up hope on Brooke, though."

After a moment, she pulled gently away to look at him. "Do you really think he took her?" This had been her deepest fear all along—that the monster who kidnapped her had her baby sister.

He leveled his gaze at her. "I think it was him, or a copycat."

She thought about all the strange and vaguely threatening things that had happened since she got there. It was obvious someone had been trying to send her a message, but was it someone who already hated her—like Sheriff Holland—who just wanted her to leave town? Or was it *him*?

She shuddered when she thought of him getting so close that he'd been in her hotel room. In her bed.

She wrapped both hands around the hot coffee mug, but not even the soothing warmth could comfort her. "I told you about the creepy 'welcome home' message someone left me at the gym," she said, and he nodded, his eyes intent on her face. "There's more that happened since then."

He looked taken aback. "Does this have something to do with the chocolates you thought I sent?"

"Yes, those were left for me at the hotel, and I just thought they were from you—because of what happened last night," she said with an averted glance.

He didn't even flash his usual grin, just seemed to

turn her words over in his mind slowly. "Missing underwear, a message on the mirror, and chocolates left at your hotel."

"Those were weird enough, but something even more disturbing happened the night we had those drinks together. When I got into bed, I could tell someone had just gotten out of it. The sheets were warm."

He jerked back in his chair, eyes wide. "Good God, Erin, why didn't you call me? How did you sleep last night?"

"I didn't. How could I? It sobered me up, and then I just sat there listening for any suspicious noises the rest of the night."

"I don't like the sound of that at all. Whoever it was would have somehow gained access to your room either via a hotel key—like through a maid—or by breaking in. I don't think you should be there alone."

Before Erin could respond, Sheriff Holland returned. For once, his ruddy face looked pale, and his eyes were haunted. She couldn't imagine it was easy to tell two parents that their son was dead, even for a callous asshole like the sheriff.

But she didn't feel sorry for him. He'd brought this all on himself when he refused to help her all those years ago, and now Steve and Brooke had paid the price.

When he walked past Adam's cubicle, Erin stood

up, hands curled at her sides. "Sheriff Holland!" He turned, his expression turning irritated when he saw who'd spoken. "Where's Rick? His ex-wife didn't know, but you're his father, and I bet you know exactly where he is. You could be withholding important information to Brooke's case by not telling us."

"Rick's got nothing to do with this," he said in a snarl.

"Yeah? Rick's the one who clearly likes young girls, who took advantage of me when I was Brooke's age. And I was kidnapped after he got fired—was that his way of seeking revenge? To pay me back for 'ruining his life' as you so idiotically claimed."

His bloated face turned thunderous. "You did ruin his life, and I'm not going to let you drag him through the mud again, acting like you're some sort of detective just because you've been palling around with one. He was a good family man before you got your claws in him."

With both of them shouting, the whole station watched unabashedly, everyone else quiet as they waited to see how Erin would respond.

It made Erin's stomach turn to hear Rick described as a good family man. She'd heard that bullshit from Norma when she was a teenager being used by her pedophile teacher, and she wasn't about to be fed that same story now.

"And just what kind of family man tries to sleep with an underage student?" she demanded.

His face turned red with anger, but they were interrupted by a commotion from the front of the station.

"Let me through! I have to talk to the sheriff!" a familiar voice shouted.

Janet barged past the receptionist with Phil at her heels.

Erin ignored them. "But you know, like father like son," she said to the sheriff. "You were no better, considering how you used to pay my mother for sex. You never kept that a secret when I'd walk by her room either."

"What the hell is going on here?" Phil demanded, but Erin whirled on him.

"You can shut your mouth. This has nothing to do with you."

Phil's face fell, like her words hurt him. Erin struggled not to roll her eyes—like she gave a shit about Phil's feelings.

"Don't talk to Phil like that! He's as desperate to find Brooke as I am," Janet said, her face wild and tear-streaked. "And here I find you yelling at the sheriff for things that have nothing to do with her disappearance!"

The anger boiled over so hot and fast that Erin didn't even think before she let her words fly. "If you and the sheriff had listened to me all those years ago, and actually done some fucking police work, then maybe the man responsible would have been caught! You could have prevented Brooke from being taken, too." She stepped closer to her mother. "Maybe if you'd actually given a shit about me, then I wouldn't have had to work all those late nights by myself, and it wouldn't have happened to me at all. Maybe if you cared as much about me as you clearly do about Brooke," she said, her voice breaking, "then all of it could have been prevented."

Janet didn't respond. Her huge eyes welled with tears, and she turned into Phil's waiting arms.

"Get her the hell out of here," the sheriff yelled at Adam, gesturing toward Erin like she was some mutt who'd wandered in off the street.

Erin didn't wait for Adam to escort her out. She'd said enough, and she knew neither her mother nor the sheriff had the virtue to admit to their own wrongdoing. She stormed out of the station with Adam following behind her, shaking from the adrenaline rush of telling off the two people who deserved it most.

23

The woods rushed by the window of Adam's SUV as Erin leaned her head against the cool glass. The branches looked sinister by the light of the moon, and she wondered what they hid. Was Brooke out there somewhere? Was she trapped in that same disgusting basement where Erin had been held?

Erin's body shook violently, and she wished she'd done more than just shouted at Sheriff Holland. His incompetence and cruelty to her as a teenager had likely made it possible for the same monster who took her to kidnap Brooke, too.

He has her, her instincts warned her. Erin was sure of it now.

"What are we going to do?" she asked Adam. "We've got to do something."

"You're going to let the police do our job."

Erin whipped her head toward Adam. "Did you not hear anything I said to the sheriff? We can't rely on him! He never helped me, and I would rather die than sit back and allow him to do nothing again."

"I didn't mean we shouldn't do anything. We just can't do much tonight. Forensics are already investigating the crime scene in the woods."

"We should go out there tonight and search the woods. See if we can find the house he kept me in. That's where Brooke is."

Adam shook his head. "We can't go out there in the middle of the night. It's too dark to find anything. First thing in the morning, I'll run a search on registered properties in that area. We can go then." He glanced over at her, sympathy warming his eyes. "You're exhausted. You're no good to me so tired you can barely keep your eyes open. Better to get some sleep and come at it fresh."

She scoffed. "I'll never be able to sleep in that room alone."

"I'll stay with you. As long as you need."

Relief bloomed through her. She wasn't sure he'd been serious when he said earlier she shouldn't be alone. "There's only an uncomfortable armchair, and you need sleep as much as me. We'll have to share the bed."

"Whatever you're comfortable with, but I'm not opposed to sleeping on the floor."

"You might not say that when you see the floor," she said with a laugh, "but I appreciate your chivalry."

Normally, Erin would be battling a tightening chest and profuse sweating at the thought of sharing a bed with a man, but tonight, she was so thoroughly exhausted that she knew she'd pass out the moment her head hit the pillow.

They parked in front of her room, and as they walked to the door, the stress of the day hit Erin so hard she stumbled over the curb. Adam caught her elbow to steady her.

"You definitely need some sleep," he said.

It felt as though she'd taken a couple of Xanax, but she knew the bone-deep fatigue was from not sleeping for over thirty-six hours. She fumbled with the key to her door and finally got it open.

Adam stopped her before she went in with a gentle hand on her arm. "Let me go first."

He went in but immediately froze.

Erin's breath caught in her throat. "Oh God, what is it now?"

"Stay there," he said and pulled out his gun.

Erin's legs turned to jelly as she waited just outside her motel room. Had someone broken in again? Was there someone in there now? Adrenaline flooded her body, making her earlier exhaustion disappear.

His sweep completed, Adam held open the door for her. His jaw muscles stood out prominently from where he gritted his teeth. "Your room is clear, but there's something you should see."

She followed him in hesitantly, her gaze scanning the room. For a moment, she didn't understand what had put him on edge.

And then she saw it: rose petals strewn all over the ugly bedspread. Her whole body shook at the thought that someone had been in her room again. As she moved closer, though, she saw an object amongst the petals. In the center of the bed lay a cheap cell phone with a handwritten message.

She inched closer to read it and nearly threw up. Her agitated mind raced forward in leaps and bounds, making disturbing connections. The message in the gym, the warm spot on her bed, the chocolates, and now this: Brooke's kidnapper had been in her room.

Her gut churned.

It could still be someone else, she thought.

But she knew.

She knew it was *him.*

Her hands shook as she grabbed the piece of paper below the cell phone.

Call me, it read.

24

E rin lurched for the phone and scooped it up. There was only one number listed in the contacts, and it was an area code she didn't recognize. Adam moved closer so he could see the screen of the phone. Her finger hovered over the send button as a sense of calm determination settled over her. She would call this asshole and find her sister.

"Don't call it yet," Adam warned. "I need to set up a trace."

He reached his hand out for the phone, but she kept it out of his reach with a sharp look. "I've seen crime shows before. That takes forever. Brooke doesn't have that kind of time."

She pressed send before he could stop her and put the phone on speaker.

The phone rang, but Erin could barely hear it over the rush of blood in her ears. Her palms were slick with sweat.

Two rings, and then three.

Pick up, dammit, Erin thought. At the same time, she didn't know if she could handle it. Hearing his voice after all these years.

Four rings.

A click on the other end made her jump. Heavy breathing filled the speaker, and Erin shivered.

"Hello, Erin," someone said in an eerily garbled tone. A modulator disguised his voice, and she gritted her teeth at the sound of it.

"Who is this?" she demanded in a much steadier voice than she thought possible.

"You know who."

Erin's heart plummeted. It was one thing for her to have suspected this, but hearing it confirmed shook her to her core. Was he doing the same to her baby sister as he had done to her?

"Is Brooke alive?" she asked, hating how her voice broke at the mention of her sister's name.

"Yes…for now," he toyed, a sickening sense of glee thick in his words.

Erin glanced at Adam, whose jaw was locked.

"What do you want? Why did you leave this phone?"

"You know the answer to that." A pause, and then the horrible voice continued. "I want you. It's always been about you, Erin. I hope you liked the chocolates I left."

Erin's skin crawled, and she had a terrible urge to hang up right then, but she resisted it. She needed to keep him talking, to get more clues, anything that might help point to his true identity. Brooke's life depended on it.

"Then why take Brooke?" she asked through gritted teeth. But she knew the answer. Deep down, she knew it the moment Adam revealed his suspicions about the cases being linked. All of it was to get to her. Her abductor, her living nightmare, wanted to finish what he started thirteen years ago.

"I want to make a trade," he said. "You hand yourself over to me, and I'll let Brooke go."

Erin glanced up in horror at Adam, who reached over and put his arm around her. She took a deep breath. Just that little bit of human contact helped. It reminded her she wasn't alone.

"How do I know Brooke's okay? I need to talk to her—for you to prove she's still alive."

There was rustling and movement in the background, and then Brooke's voice filled the small hotel room. "Erin?" she asked, her voice thin and reedy from fear.

"Brooke," Erin said in a sob. "Oh honey, oh I'm so sorry. Are you okay? I know you're not…but you're not hurt?"

"I'm not hurt, but…" Her voice broke on the last word, and Erin gripped the phone harder. She wished she could reach through the line and strangle the monster who did this to her sister. Brooke struggled to stop crying. Erin knew exactly how she felt—Brooke had been living in constant terror this whole time. It was impossible to rest, to feel at peace. Even hope began to slip away after the first few days when no one came to your rescue.

"I know, honey. I'm so sorry. We're going to get you out of there, okay? But tell me…has he touched you?"

Brooke hesitated. "No, not in that way." She lowered her voice even more. "I think he was going to. But he told me you were back in town. He's left me alone ever since."

Relief hit her like a tidal wave, nearly buckling her knees. "Everything is going to be okay. I'm going to fix this and come get you. But listen, do you know who this guy is? If I know who he is, then I can—"

"Time's up, Erin," the man's distorted voice said again.

"No, please wait!" Erin said, desperation to keep hearing her sister's voice clawing at her insides.

The man chuckled. "Don't you worry. We'll be

together soon, and then you can find out for yourself who I am. I think you'll be pleasantly surprised."

Disgust roiled through her so powerfully she had to put a hand on her stomach to steady herself. "If you let Brooke go, I'll come."

"I thought you'd say that. I'll text an address to meet me tomorrow night. Don't involve the cops, or you won't have a sister to save anymore."

Erin and Adam glanced at each other, and he nodded to encourage her to agree. For all this maniac's planning, he didn't know a cop was standing right there and had heard everything.

"I'll do whatever you want—just don't hurt Brooke."

"See you tomorrow, buttercup."

He ended the call, and with shaky hands, Erin threw the phone on the bed.

Erin had thought sleep would be out of the question after that nightmarish phone call, but by then, her body was so thoroughly exhausted, she fell asleep within minutes. Adam's presence comforted her, especially with his holstered gun at his side. He reminded her of a security guard sitting in the faded armchair, his face lit by the glow of his phone as he did research. It was the last thing she saw before she closed her eyes.

In the early morning, she woke up in a rush, choking on the scream caught in her throat. Her heart galloped away in her chest and sweat drenched her body.

"Brooke," she said, covering her face as she cried.

A warm hand touched her shoulder, and she jerked so hard she nearly fell out of bed.

"Steady there," Adam said, his voice gentle. "I didn't mean to scare you. I just wanted to let you know I'm here."

"We have to get her back, Adam," Erin said through her tears. "Tell me you have a plan."

He sat down on the edge of her bed beside her and rubbed her back as she took great, shuddering breaths. "I do have a plan."

She sensed his hesitation and looked up at him. "But what?"

He sighed and ran his fingers through his hair. "Today is going to be rough on you, but I've got your back, okay? I'm not going to let you walk into any danger."

"I'll do anything to save Brooke," she said, but she couldn't stop her body from shaking.

Suddenly, Adam pulled her in for a hug. "I'm sorry it ended up like this. That you'd be terrorized and have to face this monster. I never intended that to happen."

Erin squeezed her eyes tightly shut against new tears. "It's time I faced him. I'll do it for my baby sister."

Adam pulled back to meet her gaze. "We're going to save her, but I have to watch out for you, too." He ignored her when she shook her head in protest and continued on with his palm raised. "I've arranged for us all to meet at Janet's house. I think she deserves to know what's going on."

"That's fair," Erin reluctantly conceded.

"And just a head's up, Sheriff Holland will be there, too."

Erin stiffened. "He said no police involvement! It's enough of a risk that you know about it, much less a cop who's completely incompetent."

"I can't do this alone. I'm going to need backup, and to get that, the sheriff has to know."

Erin rubbed her arms. The whole thing sounded too good to be true: save Brooke *and* escape that monster's clutches for the second time. She was afraid to hope, but she also wasn't keen to turn herself over to him.

I'll do what I have to in order to save Brooke, she thought. She couldn't live with herself if she didn't do absolutely everything in her power to save her.

"All right," Erin said with another shuddering breath. "Let's get this over with, then." She just had to hope a visit to Janet's house with the sheriff there didn't turn into the same shit show as last time.

I n Adam's truck, they were both silent on the short drive to Janet's house. Erin tried desperately not to think of what could happen to Brooke, of the fear she'd heard when Brooke first said her name. She racked her brain over the distorted voice, knowing she'd heard it before. Of course she had. But who could it be? Rick? As a teenager, she hadn't wanted to believe he was her kidnapper. She squirmed internally when she thought of it now, but at the time, she couldn't admit to herself that someone who had told her he loved her would do something so monstrous. Still, it seemed suspicious that the sheriff refused to tell her where he was.

All during her time in that basement, she'd wondered if it could be one of Janet's "clients." She'd caught more than one watching her with a lascivious glint in his eye, like he'd rather be sampling someone a lot younger than her mother. But there were so many one-timers, men who Janet picked up in some bar from the next town over, that it could have been anyone.

She'd even wondered briefly if it was just some stranger—some opportunist. Maybe he prowled lonely highways looking for girls to kidnap, and when he saw her walking home that night with no one around to witness it, he jumped at the chance.

Until now, Erin hadn't spent a great deal of time considering who the perpetrator might be. From the moment she made her escape and it became clear justice wouldn't be served, all she cared about was getting the hell out of Huntsville. She wanted to leave everything behind, especially her time spent locked up in some psychopath's house.

Now she rubbed her forehead against the permanent headache that lived there. She should have tried harder to find his identity. Brooke was paying for her mistake now.

Before long, they arrived at Janet's house, and Erin let out an involuntary groan at the sight of Sheriff Holland's car in the driveway. Now that she knew Brooke's kidnapper was the same man who had taken her as a teenager, the blame also fell at the sheriff's feet. If he had done his damn job, this never would have happened again.

Adam knocked on the door, and Janet opened it up, her face pale and drawn. With her hair scraped back in a messy bun, she more closely resembled the Janet Erin remembered than the beautifully put-together woman she'd presented this whole time.

"Hello," she said to them both, though she didn't quite meet Erin's eyes. "Sheriff Holland is in the kitchen. I just made a fresh pot of coffee if you'd both like some."

"That would be much appreciated," Adam said.

Janet led them through her surprisingly well-decorated home and into a cozy kitchen with bright white cabinets and sparkling gray granite counters. Sheriff Holland was seated at a farmhouse table, his beefy hands wrapped around a plain white coffee mug.

"Please, sit down," Janet said, holding her hand out to the table. "I'll get you that coffee. How do you take it?"

"Just black is fine," Adam said. "Thank you."

She looked at Erin. "Would you like some, too?"

Erin was tempted to refuse. She hadn't missed how Janet seemed incapable of saying her name, but she needed coffee to chase away the fuzziness in her brain. "Yes, thank you. With a little milk or half and half if you have it."

Janet nodded and shuffled away to fix their coffees.

"Where's Phil today?" Adam asked as she added half and half to Erin's mug.

"He's at the center. He's been taking off so many days that I finally told him he needed to go in. People rely on him, and there's not much he can do here anyway." She handed them their coffees and then sat down at the table.

Erin took a sip of coffee to hide her relief. She didn't know Phil, and all she'd seen of him so far was that Janet typically turned into a weeping mess on his shoulder.

The sheriff looked up from his phone after completely neglecting to say hello to either of them. "Go ahead and start us off, Adam. I told Janet you had news for her, but I haven't shared all the details of the phone call yet."

Adam put his coffee mug down, and Janet looked at him with a combination of fear and hope on her face. "Brooke's kidnapper left a prepaid phone for Erin in her hotel room."

Janet's face crumpled. "Brooke's been kidnapped?"

"I'm so sorry, but yes, we can confirm she's been taken. Erin spoke to her, though, and she said she's not hurt."

Tearfully, Janet looked at Erin. "You spoke to her?"

"Yes, she sounded scared but okay."

"Brooke has been taken by the same man who kidnapped Erin as a teenager," Adam said, and Janet's face lost all trace of color in an instant.

Erin stared at Sheriff Holland challengingly, but he didn't even blink.

"He wants Erin, so he's willing to trade her for Brooke. He told Erin he will text her an address, and she's supposed to meet him there. Of course he warned her against police involvement."

"No," Janet said instantly and firmly. "Absolutely

not. Erin can't endanger herself like that. There has to be another way."

Erin tried not to look at her mother with her mouth hanging open. She tried to pretend like they might have the type of relationship where it wasn't absolutely shocking that she didn't want Erin to sacrifice herself to save Brooke.

"There is," the sheriff said, "and we're going to be there to protect Erin and save Brooke. No one has to get hurt."

"I've got to say, Sheriff Holland," Erin said, completely unable to ignore his calm bravado, "I'm surprised you believe me about this now. Too bad you didn't when I first approached you years ago. None of this would have happened if you had listened to me and actually done your job."

Sheriff Holland's face darkened. "Circumstances are completely different this time around. If you had—"

Erin held up her hand to stop him before it devolved into a shouting match between the two of them again. "I shouldn't have brought this up right now. The one thing we can all agree on is that Brooke is the priority. Getting her back safe is all that matters."

"That's very true," Janet said. "I'm concerned over how we're going to keep the kidnapper from knowing the police are involved. How do we know he's not watching us now?"

"That's what I've been worried about," Erin said. "What if something goes wrong? What if he hurts Brooke?"

"Things will go smoothly if we all work together," the sheriff said with a pointed look at Erin.

Adam spread his hand out on the table. "Here's what we need to do."

25

The plan, as it turned out, was to use Erin as bait with a whole police force serving as backup. If all went according to plan, they'd apprehend whoever this monster was before he even had a chance to get within range of Erin.

But as she sat in her mother's kitchen, she had her doubts it would go as smoothly as that. There seemed to be too many variables—like what if he didn't bring Brooke with him? What if he refused to tell them where she was?

What if he succeeds in taking me again? Erin thought, but then she was immediately ashamed. This wasn't the time to feel afraid for herself, not when Brooke was in very real danger.

"I'm going to make us something to eat," Janet

said, rising from the table. "Scrambled eggs and bacon okay for everyone?"

"I'm always up for bacon," Sheriff Holland said—completely unironically. Erin would have laughed, but she was too busy staring at her mother moving around the kitchen with purpose, like someone who could actually cook something more complicated than burnt toast.

"I think we should go over the map of the area again," Adam said, still focused on the plan.

Erin watched as Janet beat the eggs expertly and added herbs and spices. "I can't believe you cook now."

Janet's head whipped up to stare at Erin, and then her already red-rimmed eyes filled with tears. Erin glanced at Adam, wondering if he'd said something else about Brooke that she missed, but he and the sheriff were still looking at maps.

"I'm sorry, Erin," Janet said, her hand paused on the egg whisk. "I know I can never make it up to you, how I was during your childhood. I wasn't there when you were younger, or most importantly, when you needed me most."

Erin wasn't sure how to react—she was used to a volatile, angry Janet. Not a remorseful one.

Janet took a tentative step closer to Erin, where she still sat at the table. "I have to live with that every day, and I know our nonexistent relationship is entirely my fault. After you left, it was finally the shock I needed to get clean." She glanced at the refrigerator where there were bright, happy pictures of Brooke. "I didn't realize just how much you did for us until you were gone—how much you took care of Brooke. I swore to myself that I was going to be the mom for Brooke that I should have been the entire time—the mom I should have been for you."

Tears broke free and rolled down Janet's cheeks, but Erin didn't say anything. For a moment, she had an urge to go to her mother, but she suppressed it. They'd never had a relationship like that, and she didn't think she'd even know how. She honestly had never believed Janet would apologize to her, much less change from a drug-using prostitute into a good wife and mother. She prided herself on always knowing what to say in any PR situation, but right now, while Janet poured her heart out, she couldn't think of a single thing. Adam and the sheriff had fallen silent, too, belatedly aware that the emotional scene was taking place right in front of them.

"I never wanted to fail Brooke like I failed you, but it happened anyway, didn't it?" she asked, her voice breaking. "I failed you both the day I didn't listen to you about being kidnapped. I was terrified of the police then," she said with her gaze sliding to the cops sitting at her table, "and at the time, I wanted to sweep it all under the rug instead of deal with it. Now it's come right back to bite us in the ass, hasn't it, Sheriff?"

The sheriff's eyes widened like he was surprised at being called out by someone other than Erin. "You can't blame yourself for that, Janet. You couldn't see into the future. Hindsight is twenty-twenty."

"That's such bullshit," Erin muttered, but Adam reached over and touched her arm. *Peace,* his eyes begged.

Janet sniffled and returned her attention to Erin. "I know I failed you horribly, but I'm so proud of what you've made of yourself. You went out there and became successful even after everything you've been through. You moved to a new state and made a whole new life for yourself."

Erin swirled the dregs of her now-cold coffee around in the mug. "I don't really have a life. I have a career and a business I love, but that's it. There's only the professional side of me, and when I get home, I have nothing. No partner, no pet, not even a house plant. I go nowhere and I do nothing outside of work."

She looked out the kitchen window at the well-manicured lawn and colorful flowers. She could tell from the corner of her eye that Adam was listening to her, too. "I've never been able to escape that basement in my head. And no matter how much I try and run from it—with money or business deals or job success—it's never enough."

"Oh, Erin," her mother said, her voice heavy with what Erin belatedly realized was compassion, and it nearly brought her to tears. She couldn't remember the last time her mother had shown her the least bit of sympathy.

"That's all going to change tonight," Erin said. "I promise I'm going to bring Brooke back safe and sound, and this asshole will finally get the justice he deserves."

"If anyone can do it, it's you, Erin," Janet said, a sad smile turning up the corners of her mouth. "But I don't want you taking any unnecessary risks. That's what the police are for."

"We'll watch your six, Erin," Adam said with a serious nod.

Sheriff Holland didn't say anything, but she doubted his lazy ass was going to be anywhere near the woods tonight.

Janet met Erin's eyes, and she took a few steps toward her, arms outstretched. Instinctually, Erin's shoulders tensed, and a flash of hurt crossed Janet's face as she dropped her hands. She turned toward the bowl of eggs instead. Shame crept up on Erin, warming her cheeks. She'd never been a hugger, but for once, she didn't want to push Janet away.

"I'd love to try those eggs," Erin said with a tentative smile.

Janet beamed and immediately turned back to the stove. "Coming right up."

26

Erin spent the rest of the day in a horrible state of limbo, constantly checking the burner phone for a text. Janet told Adam and Erin to make themselves comfortable in the den, and though the TV was on, neither of them watched it. Sheriff Holland, thankfully, left shortly after eating, so at least Erin didn't have to make nice with a man she loathed.

She tried to distract herself with work—checking emails, catching up on everything she'd missed—but she found she could only focus for ten minutes at a time. Eventually she gave up and mindlessly scrolled through social media.

At five, when Phil was due to come back, Erin told Adam she wanted to go to the hotel room to shower and change. Janet had given them plenty of space, but she didn't know what Phil would do when he got home, and she wasn't up for trying to get to know him as her stepfather. Phil might be a part of Janet's new life, but Erin hadn't decided if she wanted that yet. After everything she'd been through with her mother, she didn't know if she was even capable of forgiving and forgetting. She didn't have the energy to devote to learning about a new member of her family, especially when she planned to return to New York as soon as possible.

"Let me know the second you hear something," Janet said, clutching her hands nervously at the door when they were on their way out.

"I will," Erin said. Before she could think about it, she reached out and touched Janet's shoulder. It was bony beneath her thin blouse. "It's going to be okay."

Janet nodded wordlessly and summoned a small smile. "Be safe."

When they were in Adam's truck, he gestured toward one of the fast food restaurants on their way to the hotel. "Do you want to stop and get something to eat?"

The thought of greasy fast food right now turned her stomach. "No thanks, I'm way too nervous to eat. Stop if you want something, though."

He shook his head. "I can't eat before a big operation either."

"Have you ever done something like this?"

His jaw flexed. "Once. In Chicago."

"And? Did you save the victim?" He hesitated, and she read all she needed to from his face. "Great."

"It wasn't the same type of situation—just similar. The kidnapper was in direct contact with the police for ransom, so there wasn't as good an opportunity to ambush as there is now."

That meant they didn't have bait like they did this time. Erin was sure she'd play her part well, but aside from Adam, she was concerned these cops were too stupid to pull it off. In this small town, the most complicated thing they'd ever had to deal with was maybe a few town drunks and some traffic violations.

"I trust you—it's the other cops I'm worried about," she said as they pulled into the hotel parking lot.

He turned to her after shutting off his truck. "They've agreed to follow my lead. We're going to get Brooke back safe, and nothing will happen to you, okay?"

"Okay," she said, but her stomach still tossed and turned like a ship in a storm.

Night fell in a rush of darkness, and clouds hid the moon and the stars. Erin shivered as she looked out the window of her motel room. Not even the weak lights of the parking lot could completely dispel the blackness. On edge already, when the text came at eight o'clock exactly, Erin yelped.

"Adam," Erin said, her voice coming out strangled. She stood up from where she had been sitting on the bed.

He came to her side immediately and took down the address on her screen. A hurried search on Google showed that it was a secluded part of one of the lesser-used parks just outside town—one of the areas that he and the sheriff had looked at on the map.

Another text arrived that said, *You have thirty minutes. Make sure you come ALONE. No cops.*

"Answer him and say you understand," Adam told her.

She immediately texted back, her hands shaking.

See you soon, came the response. Erin's skin crawled at the casual tone. Like she was meeting up with an old friend.

Adam gently touched her shoulder. "I'm going to leave now to get the others on my team in place. Are you okay?"

Erin felt a horrible urge to cling to him, to beg him not to leave her alone. She felt seventeen again—alone and scared. But she thought of Brooke, who really *was* seventeen and alone and scared. "I'm fine. Go ahead and go."

He nodded. When he got to the door, he turned

back. "Remember, you won't really be alone out there."

"I know," she said with a forced, brave smile.

As soon as he left, Erin collapsed back onto the bed, head in her hands. She couldn't catch her breath. Her heart threatened to burst out of her chest, and she hadn't even left her hotel room yet. A cold sweat broke out all over her body. How was she going to handle this? Already the thought of stepping outside her room gave her heart palpitations. Usually, she'd pop a Xanax and pull it together, but she didn't want anything dulling her senses. Especially when she didn't trust the cops to keep her safe.

Adam, she trusted. The rest of the police force in this town, though, had always been made up of good old boys who spent a lot of time either fishing on the job or sitting around drinking coffee. Neither of those activities inspired much confidence in their protective ability.

When she thought of Brooke in the clutches of that maniac, being dragged to some secluded meeting spot, her stomach twisted itself into knots. Would they be able to pull this off? What if something happened to Brooke—right in front of Erin? She couldn't live with herself.

She checked the time on her phone. Ten minutes had elapsed. She needed to start walking to the meetup spot. After pushing herself to the edge of the bed, she took several deep breaths.

Her body shook and sweated like she had the flu as she pushed herself out the door.

I can do this, she thought. *Just focus on Brooke.*

But the moment she was on the road out of town alone, a flood of memories hit her. She remembered the way the hair on the back of her neck stood up when she realized his truck had pulled off the road. She remembered the way her breaths came in a panicked rush when she tried to outrun him. And most of all, she remembered the feel of that rough cloth over her mouth, the darkness descending over her like the flick of a light switch.

She eyed the woods on either side of the road like a kid who was scared of lurking monsters. Erin knew the truth, though. Humans were so much worse.

The closer she came to the meeting point, the faster her heart beat in her chest, until she could feel it throbbing in her ears. To calm herself, she thought of Adam's plan. The entire woods would be surrounded, and they would narrow in once Erin got there. They would grab this guy before he ever even came close enough to talk to Erin. She tried to picture the moment he'd be arrested, when she would finally get to see who this asshole was. It almost didn't seem possible after all these years.

She arrived at the location with a few minutes to spare. The address led to one of the park's community buildings, this one on the outskirts, far from the playground and basketball courts. When Erin lived here, this had never been a safe park to go to. It was the one where drug deals went down at night, where you couldn't walk without stepping on a used condom. With only a few dim streetlights to illuminate the area, the park had a neglected feel. Instead of manicured grass, the green spaces had been overtaken by weeds and fallen leaves. The community building beside her seemed like it might fall down with the next gust of wind. She wrapped her arms around her and tried not to think about the eerie seclusion of the park at night.

Her eyes scanned the surrounding area constantly, and she checked the time every few seconds. She tried to breathe deeply and calm her racing heart. The wait crept under her skin, oppressive in its intensity. At exactly eight thirty, two figures emerge from the darkest part of the park. There wasn't enough light to tell who they were, or even if it was a man and a girl. She squinted hard into the distance, trying to make them out.

Who was it? Who had done this to her and Brooke? Warring urges inside her made her freeze in place: she wanted to run, but she also wanted to run toward Brooke to get her away from him as fast she could. Instead, she stood there with wide eyes and unsteady legs, like a terrified deer.

A cacophony of memories filled her mind so rapidly it brought on a wave of dizziness:

His big hands, reaching for her in the dark.

The grating sound of his laughter as she sobbed.

The feel of the cold floor beneath her, pressed against her spine.

Erin let out a low moan of horror.

Suddenly, frantic blurs of movement streamed from all around her. Men and women in uniform poured out of the trees, guns drawn. They descended on the two people so fast they barely had time to react, other than covering their heads with their hands. Erin's stomach felt like it was in her throat as she moved closer to see.

Bright lights flooded the area, brought in by the police on mobile carts. In an instant, Erin saw the truth. It wasn't a man and girl at all, but instead two teens—a lanky boy and a short girl, both wearing hoodies. They had matching mussed hair and flushed faces, bits of leaves and grass stuck to their clothing, like they'd just been rolling around on the ground.

Erin gaped at the scene in front of her, hand over her mouth. "No," she said breathlessly.

Where the hell was her sister? Where was the man they were actually waiting for? How had the police fucked this up so badly?

The police surrounded the terrified couple, barking questions at them while others spoke into their radios. Erin couldn't find Adam in the crowd, but at that moment, she wanted to strangle him. Had he made the call to swarm these two teenagers without waiting to first confirm their identities?

The phone in her hand vibrated, and she jumped like she'd been electrocuted. It was a text from him.

I warned you to come alone!

She closed her eyes tightly, swaying on weak legs. He was out there somewhere, watching. Her skin crawled as she turned slowly in a circle. The trees just beyond the grassy area of the park could be hiding anything. Leaves rustled gently in the breeze, and Erin imagined him hovering at the base of the trees.

It reminded her so strongly of moments trapped in the basement, when just the barest sound triggered the hair on the back of her neck to stand up. Her kidnapper had remained in the shadows, watching but not approaching. It would go on for an hour, until Erin would want to scream at him and demand that he come into the light.

The second message came right after the first, and Erin leaned over, vomiting the contents of her near-empty stomach.

You just killed your sister.

27

Erin stormed over to where the cops still surrounded the terrified teenagers. Someone grabbed at her arm, but she wrenched it away. "Adam!" she shouted. "Adam, where the fuck are you?"

She needed to talk to Adam because just looking at these incompetent morons made her want to scream at them until she went hoarse.

Another hand touched her arm, and she yanked it away with a growled, "Don't *touch* me!"

Adam put both his hands up. "I'm sorry, but I heard you yelling for me."

"I'm yelling because you promised me this would work, and all of you fucked it up! Just like I knew you would. You moved in too soon, before anyone could even tell who they were. Meanwhile, the evil bastard who has my sister was watching and saw everything! He texted me, Adam. He said he's going to kill Brooke because of *me*."

The frustration and rage built inside her until her hand itched to slap him, so she tried to turn away and leave.

"Erin, wait, please," he said, grabbing for her arm to stop her.

She whipped around and shoved him as hard as she could. To her satisfaction, he stumbled backward. As he did, a phone fell out of his pocket with a thump. It was an older model, similar to the burner phone she held in her hand. Erin's blood ran cold. She'd spent a lot of time with Adam these past few days. He had a sleek smartphone like she did.

"Whose phone is that?" she demanded, blood rushing in her ears.

"It's mine," Adam said, picking it up off the ground and replacing it in his pocket.

"The phone you've used the entire time I've been here looks nothing like that brick."

"I have two," he said calmly. "One for work and my personal one."

Erin grew silent, her mind working furiously. There was no one busier than her, and she only had one phone. How could a small town cop need two phones? Bile rose in her throat.

Adam was the one who dragged her back to Huntsville. He was the one who'd been so obsessed with her case. She had never thought of her abductor as around her age, but she never saw his face. He could have been a couple of years older. How old was Adam? She had never asked.

"Just leave me the fuck alone, okay?" she said and strode away.

Would he chase her? Would he try and stop her?

Another cop called out for Adam then, asking what to do about the teen couple. She risked a glance back to see him turn away, and then she ran.

There were hastily parked cop cars—all black and unmarked—not far from the park's community building. The moment she spotted them, she knew none of these cops would have bothered to take the keys with them.

No one was going to help save her sister. It could even be too late. She knew what that monster was capable of. The cops might have ruined their one opportunity.

Erin had to get the hell out of there.

She wrenched the door of the closest cop car open and a little chiming noise indicated the key was still in the ignition. Without hesitation, she got behind the wheel and sped out of the park.

Erin parked the police car sloppily and got out. Her mind was racing like she had just downed about five energy drinks.

Seeing Adam with that other phone threw her completely off-balance. This entire time, he was the one person she felt like she could trust, and now, she wasn't sure of anything.

She fumbled with the door to her hotel room. Once inside, she scanned the small space for any signs of intrusion, but for once, there was nothing.

With her head in her hands, she collapsed onto her bed. Were the police just morons, or had someone deliberately sabotaged the meet up? The only others who'd known were her mother and the cops. Had Sheriff Holland screwed it up to protect Rick? Was Rick the one behind all this? Or had the sheriff been covering up his own dark secrets? Erin thought of the older man coming and going out of their house when he used to pay Janet for her services. A cold shiver ran down her spine, the phantom of her abductor's touch leaving permanent fingerprints.

She got to her feet again and paced the room, unable to think straight.

It all came back to Adam. He was the one who brought her here, who arranged this ambush. He was the one calling the shots, which meant that he must have told the others to move in on those teenagers without making sure who it was. Was it another colossal screwup like the one he told her about in Chicago? Or deliberate?

She shook her head. She didn't want to believe that of Adam. She didn't want to believe she'd been so thoroughly duped by a guy she trusted to truly be on her side. One of the only people in this wretched cesspool of a town to believe Erin had been telling the truth all those years ago. She shuddered all over when she thought about kissing him now. Surely if he'd been the man who'd held her hostage thirteen years ago, she would have sensed something. But who was really behind all this? Someone else she hadn't considered yet? A stranger?

Either way, Erin had been an idiot to trust the Huntsville police. She knew they were incompetent from personal experience, and now her baby sister would pay the price.

Suddenly, Erin came to a stop in the middle of the room. The cops were incompetent, yes, but something else struck her with a lightning bolt of horror. He never intended to show up.

That bastard had been watching her the entire time —he made that clear with all of his little visits. The gym. The motel room. He always knew when she'd be out, and he could leave evidence of his visits behind. No doubt he also had seen her tagging along with Adam all over town. With the cops—and Adam—

investigating Brooke's disappearance, the kidnapper would be an idiot to believe they wouldn't get involved in a trade-off.

He had set Erin up as another one of his games to fuck with her head.

"Oh God, Brooke," she said, breaking down into painful sobs. Where was she? What was happening to her? Adam had told her that the girls who went missing after Erin were never seen again. Now, the same thing would happen to Brooke.

What could she do to stop it? Was it too late already?

She cast her eyes around the room, looking for anything that might help, and her gaze landed on the bottle of pills. If Brooke was already dead, then she didn't want to live anymore. She couldn't with that guilt. It would eat her alive, and she'd be better off in the ground than living with it every day of her life.

If this had only ever been a setup, that meant the kidnapper never intended for Erin to find Brooke. Erin wrapped her arms around her middle as though she would tear in half. She would never see her baby sister again. She hadn't bothered to see her in all the years since she left, and now she'd never have the chance.

The sobs turned uncontrollable, and she couldn't catch her breath. Before she could think about it, she grabbed the bottle of Xanax.

Shaking out the pills into her hand, she kept going

until every last one fell out of the bottle. She could end this pain now. Maybe even join her sister.

No more dealing with past trauma, or panic attacks, or kidnappers from hell.

Just peace.

The voice of hopelessness rang out loud and clear in Erin's mid, but another part of her whispered other things. Pills were uncertain. She could wind up on a ventilator in a hospital somewhere, still alive. And unable to fight back.

Whispers in her head increased in volume until they shouted that Brooke might still be alive. If Erin killed herself now, she would have abandoned her sister again, this time permanently.

She thought of Brooke's voice on the phone, scared and broken. No one had come to save Erin when she'd been trapped. She wouldn't wish that crippling despair on anyone, least of all her sister.

How would she find Brooke now though?

But then she remembered: the kidnapper had given her a phone. She could call him and beg for Brooke's life. Offer herself in trade like he wanted—for real this time. For one horrible moment she held the pills in her hand and debated with herself. She froze in a state of paralysis, her mind imagining terrible things. If she called, would he say Brooke was already dead? Would she hear Brooke scream?

Her phone rang, and she jumped like a startled cat,

her heart pounding. It wasn't the phone he gave her, though. It was her other phone. She answered it without even looking at the caller ID.

"Hello?" she asked breathlessly.

"Oh, thank God!" a familiar, and completely unwelcome, voice said.

"Mr. Roland," Erin said, irritation bleeding heavily into her tone. To talk to him now on top of everything else was unthinkable. Impossible.

"Erin, I've been simply desperate to get in touch with you. You would not *believe* the colors in this ad. They're muted and boring and offensive, and I simply can't stand them. What we need is—"

"How did you get my personal number?" Erin practically growled into the phone.

He tittered, and her skin crawled. "I just called around until—"

"My little sister could be dead! Fuck you, and fuck your ad colors!" she shouted and before he could respond she threw the phone where it smashed against the wall.

Breathing hard, she used her pumping adrenaline to scoop up the burner phone. She didn't stop to think. She just hit dial.

He answered on the first ring, like he'd been expecting her.

"I was wondering if you'd call me," he said, and Erin recoiled away from the phone. "You didn't follow the rules. You had the cops there waiting for me, and that made me very angry. I think you remember what I'm like when I get angry."

Erin shuddered against the memory that fought to emerge. She couldn't lose herself to the trauma of her past. Brooke needed her. "It was a mistake to involve the cops. I see that now. I'm so sorry, but I still want to make that trade."

He fell silent for a moment, and she pressed the phone to her ear so hard it hurt. Was this when he said she was too late? Brooke was already dead?

"No cops," he said, and she let her breath out in a rush.

"No cops this time. Just me for Brooke. Is she okay? Is she alive?"

"She's alive, but you can't talk to her," he said in that eerie distorted voice. Erin sagged with relief. "The time for that is over. If you try anything, then I'll kill her, and they'll never find the body. I'll leave it to rot somewhere, picked at by animals and insects so you'll never have a nice grave site to visit. You'll never have a body to bury."

Erin closed her eyes and swallowed hard against the rising vomit in her throat. "I swear I won't tell anyone. I just want her to be okay. I'll do anything you want as long as you free her."

"I want you to come back to our special place."

Erin shook all over, but she nodded. "I'll do it. Just tell me how to get there."

"I'll send you directions. Follow them carefully, and remember, don't share them with anyone, or you'll arrive just in time to see your sister die."

"No one else. Just me. Please don't hurt her," Erin said, her voice breaking.

"That's up to you," he said and hung up.

For a moment, Erin couldn't move. Where before she had only thought she would see her kidnapper face to face, now she knew for sure. Now she would walk straight into his house of terrors and pray that he would trade her for Brooke.

Old symptoms of a panic attack reared their heads —tight chest, dots on the edges of her vision. She didn't have time for this. *Just take one step at a time,* she told herself. That was all she had to do. Just baby steps.

She grabbed her bag and put the phones and keys inside. Her vision darkened as she walked toward the door, and for a moment, she swayed, one hand on the door frame. She hadn't eaten since the scrambled eggs this morning, but anything she tried to down now would only come right back up.

Slowly, she made her way to the stolen cop car to wait for the directions, sweat pouring from her body. She gritted her teeth against the fear that threatened to rattle her apart. This might all be for nothing. Brooke might already be dead, and she could be walking into her worst nightmare. She couldn't trust the police though. Not after what happened.

She couldn't trust anyone.

It had to be her.

The directions arrived, and as Erin expected, it had her driving on a path deep in the woods. The house that had tormented her dreams for years. The one with the basement.

She gripped the steering wheel hard. For too long, she'd been trapped in that house in her mind, unable to break free. She was sick of it. Sick of the dreams, the panic attacks, and all her fruitless effort to move on.

She may have been walking into this alone, but she wasn't a seventeen-year-old girl anymore. She was strong, physically fit, and seriously pissed off.

It was time to end this, once and for all.

28

His directions took her on the main road that went past Eddie's, and she couldn't help but think of that fateful night when she walked home from the diner for the last time. Now, she turned off onto a road barely wide enough for two cars. It cut through the woods, weaving between the looming trees. Her breathing sounded labored, like she'd run five miles. All she wanted to do was push the car to its limit and drive as fast as she could to get to Brooke. Like being trapped in a nightmare, she couldn't go much faster than a crawl on the twisty road. The headlights cast obscure shadows around her, the trees so thick and canopied that she couldn't see the night sky.

Another mile, and then she turned off onto a dirt road she wouldn't have noticed if she hadn't been looking for the abandoned tractor mentioned in the directions. No street sign revealed its location, and it was partially hidden by trees and forest undergrowth. As the car's suspension shook over the rough road, her heart sank at the thought that this was the type of place no one would ever find.

Forced to drive the car at a crawl, her teeth were gritted so hard her jaw hurt. Fog obscured her vision, preventing her from seeing more than a few feet in front of her at a time. At last, she arrived in a little clearing, in the midst of which was a horribly dilapidated cabin, just as she remembered it from her nightmares. Kudzu twined over half of it, weakening the front porch to the point that a strong breeze might make it collapse. Rust had eaten up the tin roof. From this vantage point, she couldn't see the basement window where she'd made her escape, and she wondered if it had been boarded up.

She parked the car and stepped out into wisps of fog that curled around her legs. The open front door revealed a yawning darkness like an open grave, and she shivered. With one hand still on the car door, she stood still, watching and listening. No sounds or movements came from within the house, but the goosebumps covering her skin told her someone watched her.

Her legs refused to move.

Brooke, she told herself. *Think of Brooke.*

The inky blackness of the inside of the house, though…no way could she walk in there blind. She had a cop car, though. There had to be emergency supplies like a flashlight. She dug around in the center console first and then the glove compartment until she found a heavy metal flashlight.

The flashlight's heft comforted her as she walked through the door and into her past. The smell hit her first: damp earth and rotten leaves. Beneath her feet, the floor had disappeared under a thick layer of filth, dirt and rotting vegetation. Some of the kudzu had burst through the back windows, too, slowly taking over the cabin.

She walked slowly and cautiously, but her panting breath and the creaking floorboards made it obvious to anyone who might be listening where she was.

Just beyond the doorway lay the living room, and Erin swept the flashlight's beam over the space. Nothing here, only creeping vegetation and a distinct lack of furniture that rendered it unusable. A door lay to her left. The basement entrance? Slowly, she turned the knob, flinching as she opened it.

An empty closet.

Letting out her breath in a rush, she crept deeper into the house. A furtive noise came from the kitchen just ahead, and she stopped, hand gripping the flashlight. She listened hard, but her own heartbeat in the quiet space seemed to drown out any sound.

She didn't want to investigate, but she had to find her sister.

She made herself count to three.

Adrenaline flooded her so much her teeth chattered as she inched around the corner, flashlight raised.

The light revealed a primitive kitchen, with a filthy, rust-stained sink and potbellied stove. The sound came again: a soft rustling from behind a narrow door. What if Brooke was tied up in there?

Holding her breath, Erin pulled open the door.

She yelped as her flashlight's beam reflected off a pair of beady rat eyes. The rodent sat on a ripped-open box of crackers, baring its teeth before she slammed the door shut.

She spun on her heel to get the hell out of the rat-infested kitchen. As she started to walk away, she saw it: a heavy metal door with a deadbolt.

When she'd been a prisoner here, she'd never seen this side of the door. Still, she knew where it led.

There was only one place Brooke could be.

The flashlight's beam jumped as Erin's hand trembled, but the door offered no resistance. It opened with a creak that dragged Erin back to all the moments she'd huddled down below, listening for that tell-tale sign he was coming.

She almost couldn't do it. The thought of walking herself down into her former prison made her stand there in a stupor.

But then she thought of Brooke down there alone and scared.

And she took the first step.

The stairs led down into the dark, and as they creaked and protested Erin's every footstep, she had to resist the urge to fly down them like a kid running from imaginary monsters. Here, she knew they weren't imagined.

When she reached the bottom, she turned right, instinctively moving toward where she'd once been held against her will. Her heart pounded, and she flinched at every shadow.

Deep in the gloom of the basement, Brooke sat blindfolded, her mouth covered with duct tape on a decrepit chair near the window Erin had escaped through. As she expected, the window had been boarded up. Brooke's head hung down with her chin on her chest, and for a terrible moment, Erin thought the worst.

"Brooke!" Erin whispered loudly into the quiet space.

Brooke jerked her head up at the sound, and tears sprang to Erin's eyes as she rushed to her side. Rope bound her to exposed pipes in complicated-looking knots. Brooke's cheek had a dark bruise across it, but she seemed otherwise unhurt. Her clothes were filthy, and it looked like she hadn't bathed, which Erin knew from experience was a good sign. He hadn't hurt her or touched her in the many ways he did to Erin, and she nearly cried with relief.

She threw the flashlight down and hurriedly untied the blindfold. When Brooke finally met her gaze, her eyes filled with tears. She struggled to speak, but of course any words were muffled under the tape.

Erin gently tugged at the duct tape, but it held fast, and Brooke winced as it tore at the sensitive skin of her face.

"I'm so sorry, Brooke," Erin said, "I'm going to get you out of here."

Brooke's eyes widened, and she struggled against her bonds.

"I'm hurrying," Erin told her, fighting the tape.

The moment the tape ripped off, Brooke shouted, "Erin, behind you! He's here!"

Erin whipped around and froze when she finally came face-to-face with the kidnapper.

29

E rin stared at her abductor with paralyzing confusion. Her brain moved in slow motion as she took him in.

"Phil?"

Phil. Her mother's husband. Brooke's stepfather.

Erin frowned, lost for words. No, this didn't make sense. Janet married Phil after Erin left Huntsville. She'd never met him before coming back to town when Brooke went missing.

Phil smiled at her, his dark eyes intense. "I missed you so much, Erin. I can't tell you how many times I've thought about you being back here with me. It's been so hard not to say anything to you—not to reach out and touch you when you were right there, in my house."

Erin took a step back, putting more distance

between herself and Phil. Was he insane? Did he think he knew her?

His smile slipped from his face. "You didn't know it was me," he said, a clear note of hurt in his tone. He patted his protruding stomach. "I understand though. I've changed a lot since we were last together."

Erin tried to think back. The man who'd taken her had never shown his face, but he had been much thinner than Phil was now. He'd been average height, just like Rick, which was why she'd never discounted the possibility it had been her old English teacher. And he'd always worn the mask. In the dark of the basement, even his eye color had been obscured.

She stared at Phil now, who watched her with the disturbing intensity of a starving wolf. She'd seen that before. She thought of how Janet said he worked at the community center, where she got clean and got her act together. Her mind cast back through her memories, and suddenly, she remembered. She *had* seen Phil before. That day after she'd been so thoroughly embarrassed at church. When that alcoholic came up to them and told her mother about the AA meetings at the community center.

He had been skinny with wild, scraggly hair back then. Now he was heavy-set and bald, but they both shared that disturbingly intense look. She could see the man he used to be within the heavier frame.

Phil's eyes lit up. "You remembered, didn't you? I knew you would."

"Why did you do this?" Erin said, gesturing toward Brooke, who remained tied up behind her.

"It was never about her—it was always about *you*. You're probably upset with me, thinking I was trying to replace you, but you have to know that isn't true. From the very first moment I saw you, I knew we were meant to be together." His eyes glazed over at the memory, and Erin recoiled.

"There you were in church, with your short skirt and your long legs. The sunlight made your hair glow like you were some kind of angel. I knew someone as young and beautiful as you would never talk to someone like me, so I approached your mom instead. I knew she'd talk to anyone, especially men."

Erin's skin crawled at the shared memory. It sickened her to think that this perverted maniac had watched her from the back of the church on one of the worst days of her life.

"But your mom didn't come to those meetings, at least not then, so I had to take matters into my own hands. I followed you around, got to know your routine—you really worked late!—until one night, I finally had everything ready for us to be together." He stared straight into her eyes like a man confessing his undying love, and it chilled Erin down to her marrow. "I longed for you, and I finally had you. When you left, I never stopped longing for us to be together again."

"I didn't leave—I escaped," Erin said, disgust creeping into her tone despite her effort to sound neutral and keep him calm.

He didn't hear her, or if he did, he was too lost in his sick romantic fantasy to acknowledge what she said. "I'm so glad you've come back. You know, I tried to move on with other girls. I always brought them here to our special place on our anniversary, but it was never the same. They weren't *you*. You've always been the girl who got away."

Erin blanched at the mention of other girls. "Where are the others?"

"I don't want you to worry about them. They meant nothing to me. They couldn't hold a candle to my love and passion for you. They were just a temporary relief, and when I was done, I burned them out back."

Behind her, Brooke whimpered. Bile rose in Erin's throat as she contemplated the full meaning of what he'd so casually said. Eleven girls. All of them tortured by this man. All of them dead.

Erin wanted nothing more than to make him stop telling her these things. She had this intense urge to grab her sister and run. But as horrible as it was to hear the truth, she had to keep him talking until there was an opportunity to get Brooke out of there.

"Why did you marry my mother?" The sick son of a bitch had wheedled his way into her mother's life.

Phil gave her a look. "I thought it would be obvious. I wanted to be close to you. I thought surely you'd come home to see your family, but you never did. After you left me, I thought I could settle for the next best thing—Janet was your mother after all. I knew once she got cleaned up there would be a strong resemblance. And once she started taking care of herself, it did help. But it wasn't enough. It was never enough."

Nausea crashed down over her so strongly she tasted acid at the back of her throat. The man who had kidnapped her as a teenager had married her mother. He pretended Janet was her, and when that hadn't been enough, he found and murdered other girls. All because they weren't Erin.

Erin rocked back on her heels, her powerful imagination supplying the rest against her will. Phil and her mother in bed, Phil picturing Erin instead. Phil watching Brooke as she grew into a beautiful young woman. Phil preying on his own stepdaughter.

She had to get them out of here. Now.

Phil blocked the way back to the stairs, and with the window boarded up, it was the only exit. They'd have to get around him. But how could she free Brooke from her ropes fast enough? She needed something to hit him with—something to knock him out. Why the hell had she put that heavy flashlight down?

Erin scanned the area behind Brooke, judging the distance between them and the flashlight. She'd never turned it off, so its beam still illuminated the basement floor and a shadowy back corner. Her stomach dropped. Phil stood mere feet from them, but the flashlight had to be ten feet or more away.

She bit back a scream at the fucked-up level of manipulation on display here, but she had to keep him talking. Maybe if she distracted him, she could pivot herself close enough to grab the flashlight. "I understand about my mother," Erin said, though she couldn't let herself think about the full implications again. "But what about Brooke? You said she was your daughter. How could you do this to your own family?"

Phil shook his head slowly, like a dog who hears a painfully high-pitched sound. "I never thought about Brooke like that. At first. But the more she grew up, the more she began to look like you."

Erin could see it—Brooke looked just like she did at seventeen, when Phil took her and broke her forever. But Phil hadn't been Erin's stepfather. She hadn't watched him marry her mother or get up every morning to fix him his coffee. He hadn't lived in her *house*. A fierce, protective rage rose in Erin then, her whole body thrumming with the need to beat this monster to a pulp. She wouldn't let him continue to traumatize her sister.

"I tried to fight it—I really did. But I couldn't help

myself." He shrugged almost sheepishly, as though he was confessing to eating too many donuts instead of kidnapping his own stepdaughter. "I was out driving around, looking for my next girl. That's when I saw Brooke and Steve leaving Eddie's. It was so perfect, Erin—it was just like the night I brought you home. She had her hair down and over her shoulder—just like you used to wear it."

He glanced over at Brooke now, and she flinched away from his attention. Revulsion filled Erin so deeply she feared she wouldn't be able to hide it in her expression anymore. She no longer wanted to just beat him. She wanted him *dead.*

"And then what happened?" Erin said, trying to draw him away from Brooke. But every time she moved even an inch toward the flashlight, he shifted his bulk to block her. He looked out of shape, but he was only a few feet away from them. He could catch her easily.

"I watched and waited. Steve stopped on the side of the road, almost in the woods, and it was so perfect. It was almost exactly where I'd taken you with me that night. They were there for some alone time, so I knew they wouldn't even hear me coming. I slipped on my ski mask and pulled open Steve's car door first—it wasn't even locked. He had his hands all over Brooke, and she looked just like you, so I lost my head a little bit. He fought me, so I had to kill him. Brooke tried to fight me off, too, but she was no match for a little chloroform-soaked hankie."

Brooke made a strangled noise behind her, and then she started crying. Erin burned with the need to go to her sister and comfort her, but she didn't dare move. The way Phil told his story struck Erin as disturbingly nonchalant and completely without remorse. He had murdered Brooke's boyfriend right in front of her, and then kidnapped her. Maybe she could catch him off guard somehow and make a run for the flashlight.

As if he knew where her attention had shifted, Phil took a step closer. "You know, I never meant to keep her for long. I just wanted to relive that first night I was with you—just for a moment. But then that hotshot cop from Chicago said he planned to meet with you and talk you into coming back to town—he'd been snooping around, trying to figure out the connection of those other girls. And he knew it had something to do with you. So when I heard you might be coming back, it changed everything. I knew I could use Brooke to get you here."

"And now you can let her go," Erin said, trying to keep her voice strong and reasonable. It sounded thin and reedy to her ears. "You have me here, and the sooner you let her go, the sooner we can be alone together. Just like it was before."

Brooke made a small noise behind her, and Erin flinched, willing her in her mind to keep quiet.

Phil gave her a pitying look. "I'm afraid I can't do that. Brooke has seen my face, and now she knows who has been behind all this. Unfortunately, there's only one way this plays out: with you both dead." He looked regretful for a moment. "That doesn't mean we can't have our alone time, but I'll have to put Brooke out of her misery first."

30

E rin had taken enough self-defense classes to know never to take her eyes off her attacker. Now that she thought back to all the times she'd practiced, she realized she'd always pictured fighting back against the man who'd taken her. However, the Phil who'd taken her had been half the size of the one who stood before her now. Twice her size, he could easily crush her. If she waited passively for him to attack, he could overpower her just by throwing his weight around. She had to strike first.

With no weapon, though, it was like squaring off against a bear. He would bat her aside like an annoying fly.

Suddenly, the magnitude of what they faced if she failed hit Erin so hard she nearly crumbled under the weight of it. Phil would kill them both, but before they died, he'd probably torture them. He knew the greatest torment for Erin would be to watch something terrible happen to Brooke. Erin couldn't think of anything more horrific than watching Brooke be killed in front of her.

As she prepared her body for the fight of her life, a hyperawareness descended on her. Her muscles, starved for food after days of barely eating, quivered with weakness. A fuzziness coated her vision and thoughts, like she'd taken a few Xanax after all. Worst of all, her mind conjured up a flood of memories of the things this man had done to her. Of what he would most certainly do again, but this time, to her and her sister.

Drenched in sweat, Erin summoned her strength.

B efore he could move, she rushed forward and landed a powerful kick into his sternum. He doubled over instantly, gasping for breath. She landed punches on the back of his head and neck with her fist in the motion of a hammer. He stumbled to his knees.

Immediately, she whirled toward Brooke and went to work on her ropes. The knots were strong, and the adrenaline coursing through her body made her fingers shake. Erin managed to free Brooke's hands, and then her sister desperately tried to help her with the rest of the rope.

Before she could make any more progress, Phil grabbed hold of Erin's hair and yanked her head back. Brooke screamed, and Erin tried to fight him off. To keep him from scalping her, she had to hold onto her hair. His strength quickly overpowered her. She screamed as a huge chunk of her hair tore free. He stumbled back, still clutching her hair as blood rolled down Erin's face.

She rolled away, whimpering in pain as she tried to get to the flashlight.

He came at her again, trying to grab her with his meaty hands. She kicked again and managed to shove him back. With a roar, he raced toward her before she could even catch her breath. She blocked his punches as best she could, but the power and rage behind every blow knocked her two steps back.

He landed blows on her ribs, and the bones gave way under his assault. Erin shouted in agony, clutching her side. Horror dawned on her as she struggled to limp away: this was nothing like her self-defense classes. He didn't stand still like a punching bag. He was real and far more deadly than anything she expected.

· · ·

"You're never leaving me again!" Phil yelled at her, his voice distorted from his physical exertions.

He charged her again, and this time, she didn't move fast enough. His big body crashed into hers, knocking her to the hard basement floor. The air left her lungs in a rush, and she floundered. Fists flying, he landed punch after punch on Erin's body, the sound of bone hitting flesh deafening in her ears. She screamed as he hit her already broken ribs, as he bruised sensitive organs. She struggled to fight back, but she could no sooner push him off than if he'd tied her down. He landed a blow to her face that caused her eye to instantly swell shut, blocking her vision.

He'll never stop. I'm not strong enough to fight him.

Suddenly, Brooke was there, tugging his broad shoulders in an attempt to pull him off her. Some of the ropes still dragged behind her. It distracted Phil just long enough for Erin to draw a breath into her lungs. Phil viciously backhanded Brooke. Erin screamed as her sister fell to the floor in a heap.

Erin scrambled to her feet as Phil loomed over her. She raised her arm to block another punch, her whole body screaming in protest. He just kept coming.

Erin curled in on herself, exhaustion hitting her limbs so strongly her legs threatened to collapse any moment.

"That's right," Phil said with a grin as he grabbed hold of her, "just give up. You can't fight me. You never could."

His grin disappeared when they both heard something in another part of the basement. Heavy footsteps on the wooden steps. A dark-haired man in a blue uniform appeared, flashlight piercing the gloomy room. Phil jerked his head toward the bottom of the stairs. Erin cried out when she saw Adam. She didn't know how he knew to come here, but all that mattered now was that he had a gun.

He had the gun drawn, but before he could use it, Phil grabbed hold of Erin and shoved her toward Adam so forcefully that she collapsed at his feet. In the confusion, Phil rushed Adam. Enraged and wild, he began pummeling Adam with his thick fists. The gun went flying off into the shadows of the basement.

Adam put up a fight, but Phil had a weight advantage, and a wild fury that could not be stopped. He threw himself into Adam, using elbows and fists, shoving Adam into the wall with back-breaking force.

Erin crawled to Brooke's side and helped her sit up. "I'm with you now, whatever happens," she told her.

A sickening crack, and then Erin watched in horror as Adam slid to the floor. Phil had grabbed Erin's dropped flashlight and swung it into Adam's head, knocking him clean out.

With Adam down, her hope that they would get

out of this alive dwindled to nothing. Still, she couldn't just give up and let him do whatever sick things he had planned for them.

Phil panted hard, sweat and blood running down his face. Like a scene from a nightmare, he turned toward them again. Erin summoned her flagging strength and tried to get to her feet.

"Run, Brooke!" she shouted, giving her little sister a shove.

Erin charged toward Phil, throwing her whole weight into as they collided. She threw punches and kicks, but a child could hit harder at this point. He blocked them and laughed in her face. She drew her knee up rapidly, attempting to take him by surprise and hit him in the balls. But he shoved her back so hard she lost her balance and crashed to the floor.

He leapt on top of her, his weight crushing. His hands went around her throat and squeezed.

She thrashed violently against him, but it only gained her an inch of breathing room.

"You're feistier now, and I like that," he said through teeth clench with the effort to pin her down and choke her. She continued to throw her weight against him, managing a few gasps of air here and there. "But I've never been a patient man. Thirteen years has been an eternity. And let me tell you a little secret," he said and leaned close to her ear, his fetid breath washing over her face. "It doesn't matter if you're alive or dead. So long as I have your body."

His words reverberated through her, so horrifying that she was in danger of losing control of her bladder.

With an evil grin, he squeezed his hands harder around her throat.

Dark spots appeared at the edges of her vision as she weakly tried to push him off her.

I'm going to die.

She cast her gaze around to see if Brooke had at least made it out of there.

"Erin!" her sister screamed, and she sounded close —too close. Why hadn't she gotten the hell out of there when she told her to?

And that was when Erin saw the gun.

It had spun away during the fight, and now it lay mere inches away. She stretched her arm out toward it. Her fingertips brushed the very edge of the cold metal. It remained just out of reach.

Her lungs screamed for air.

She struggled against him, tears tracking down her face at her effort. If she could just inch closer…

With the last of her strength, she thrashed powerfully, drawing her knees up and stretching her arm out at the same time. Nothing happened. She couldn't move even a millimeter from underneath him.

Suddenly, Brooke stood above Phil, holding the

police flashlight high. She brought it down with a thud against the back of Phil's head.

He roared with pain and let go of Erin's throat.

With a huge lurch, Erin reached toward the gun. Her hand closed around the cold metal.

She shoved the muzzle of it against his ribs. He froze, hands slackening on her throat. Erin took in great gulps of breath and pushed the gun even harder into his soft flesh.

Slowly, Phil removed his hands.

"Get the fuck off me," she said between violent coughs. Her throat burned.

He heaved himself off her, and she stumbled to her feet, swaying as the blood returned to the rest of her body. She kept hold of the gun and pointed it at his chest.

"You're mine," he said. "You've always been mine."

Before she could react, with head lowered like a bull, he charged at her.

For a big man, he moved fast, and Erin's reactions were slowed by her brush with death. They grappled for control of the gun.

Brooke screamed and screamed.

And then, in the midst of the chaos, the explosive bang of the gun was deafening.

31

As the sound reverberated in the small space of the basement, it took Erin a moment to realize what had happened. Still holding the gun, she scrambled away from Phil. His face was an ugly mask of impending death. Red bloomed across his stomach. A gut shot that would likely kill him slowly, which was exactly what he deserved. Still, Erin had watched enough horror movies to know that the bad guy could still make a miraculous recovery.

She raised the gun again.

"You'll always be mine," he said as he took a shaky step toward her.

Erin's lip curled in disgust. "I'll never be yours," she said and shot him again in the head.

He slumped to the floor like a ton of bricks, his eyes

open and unseeing. Blood poured out of the back of his head, and Erin turned away.

She limped to Brooke's side and gingerly wrapped her arms around her sister, her bruised ribs and battered body sending out shooting pains of agony in protest. They collapsed into each other and sank to the floor of the basement. Brooke was shaking uncontrollably, but she hugged Erin back.

"I'm so sorry—for everything," Erin said, tears falling fast and hard now that they were finally out of danger. "I should have figured it out before now, and then I could have stopped that from happening to you."

The idea that Brooke would suffer what Erin had for the past thirteen years tore her apart.

Brooke had tears running down her face, too. "You can't blame yourself for what he did. It was Phil. He tricked us all."

Erin glanced over at his body. "Thank God he's dead. He's dead, and he can't hurt any of us ever again."

A groan came from another part of the basement, and Erin got painfully to her feet when she realized it was Adam. She hurried over to him and helped him up.

He had a nasty egg on the side of his head, one that was worryingly close to his temple. Blood poured from the wound. He held onto her arms to steady himself, looking around the room with a dazed expression.

When he got a good look at Erin, though, he wrapped his arms around her. "What the fuck did he do to you?"

"Well, he's dead, and we're not," she said, her voice a mere croak. "That's what matters."

Adam's grimace deepened. "Your throat looks horrible." He reached out and barely grazed her hair with his fingertips. "You're bleeding."

"You are, too," she said. "The bastard ripped my hair out." She winced. "I think some of my ribs are broken, too."

Brooke walked over to them, and Adam turned to her. "Brooke, thank God. Are you okay?"

She gingerly touched her bloodied lip and nodded.

Adam pulled out his phone. "I'm going to call for an ambulance to check both of you over—"

"And yourself," Erin said, reaching up gently to touch the lump on his head.

"I'm not proud that I got knocked out so fast, but yes, I'll get checked out, too."

After he called for backup and an ambulance, he went and examined the body. Brooke and Erin watched from the base of the stairs, arms around each other.

As he squatted down beside what was left of Phil, he glanced back at Erin with a tortured look. "I'm sorry I didn't pull the trigger fast enough, but I'm glad you did. Saves us the mess of a trial when honestly, this evil bastard deserves to be in the ground."

"Agreed," Erin said with a shudder.

When he rejoined them at the base of the stairs, Erin thought about how hidden away they were. "How did you know to find us here?"

He gave her a pointed look. "You stole a police car. They all have tracking devices in them, so when I first noticed it missing and saw it was at your hotel, I figured I'd just meet up with you later. But next time I checked, you were deep in the woods, and it didn't take much to figure out where you'd gone." He clenched his jaw. "I don't think I've ever been so terrified, Erin. It was worse than Chicago. Because if anything had happened to you…" he trailed off and cleared his throat. "I got here as fast as I could, but even that wasn't much help. Trust me, I'm dying inside that he got the jump on me."

"Your gun was plenty helpful," Erin said with a nod toward Phil's dead body.

"Ouch," Adam said, clutching his chest. "Well, at least something did its job. Now let's go outside to wait. I'm sure you don't want to be down here another second, Brooke."

Brooke flashed him a grateful look, and they all headed back upstairs, the steps illuminated by Adam's flashlight.

Once outside, Brooke took deep breaths of the fresh air while Erin watched her sympathetically. She remembered the moment she was finally free of the revolting smells of the basement, how deliciously sweet the air outside seemed.

"I should have never left you for so long," Erin said, watching this girl that was nearly an adult. She could barely see the four-year-old sister she'd left behind in her face.

Brooke turned toward her, expression soft. "I never blamed you for leaving. I still remember the days you'd been missing and the night you came home. You gave me some excuse about being lost in the woods, and I accepted that when I was four. When I got older, though, I knew something terrible had happened to you. You were a ghost of who you were before—you couldn't even sleep anymore."

Erin looked at her in shock. "I didn't know you noticed—you were so little at the time."

Brooke shrugged. "I could still tell something was wrong. Sometimes I'd wake up, and I'd find you just staring out the window. I used to fall asleep watching you and wondering what you were looking for." She rubbed her arms as if to ward off a chill. "Now I think I know."

Erin knew exactly what she was talking about. The nights spent terrified that her kidnapper would come for her. The only way she could ease her anxiety would be to keep watch at the window.

"I always meant to come back for you, though," Erin said. "But then the timing never seemed right. I was in college and then an internship and then working…and when I'd look at your pictures, you always seemed so happy. I convinced myself you'd be okay."

"I have been happy," Brooke said with a sad smile, no doubt struggling to rectify the truth about her step-father in her mind. "Mom got better soon after you left. I don't remember the bad times very well now—they're more like hazy memories. But you know, you could have called. I've always missed you terribly."

Tears prickled Erin's eyes. "I know. I'm so sorry. It's my own damn fault—this guilt I carried. It was one thing to worry in the back of my mind that Janet might still be using and drinking and everything else, but I knew it would change everything if I spoke to you and you asked me for help. So I never called; I never opened that door. I was selfish. So selfish."

Brooke reached out and touched her arm. "You had a horrible thing happen to you at a young age, and you're not my mom, Erin. It wasn't up to you to raise me. I have a mom who actually stepped up when I needed her. But I really missed my sister."

Erin broke down and Brooke hugged her tightly. "Anyway, you saved me now, so how could I blame you for anything else?" Brooke said with a teary smile. "The important thing is that it's over."

Erin hugged her back. "We're safe, and we're free of that monster. He'll never hurt us—or anyone else —again."

Talking to Brooke after all this time was like having a terrible weight Erin didn't even know she'd been carrying lifted off her shoulders. Like being able to take a deep, restorative breath for the first time since she was seventeen. And now the man that had haunted her for her entire adult life was dead. Erin waited for shock to set in—shock that she had taken a life. But it didn't. All she felt was relief. He could never hurt anyone again.

She couldn't undo the damage Phil had done—to her and to Brooke—but now that he was dead, she thought she finally had a chance to move on and have a healthy, full life.

She was sure as hell going to try.

32

A couple of hours later, Erin, Brooke, and Adam were all in beds at the local hospital. The ER was so small that the beds were next to each other, separated by ugly blue curtains. After their tests were completed, they'd drawn the curtains back so they could all talk to one another. Brooke and Adam both had concussions from Phil hitting them in their heads. The doctor told Adam he was lucky. A centimeter to the right, and the blow to his temple might have killed him.

Erin had never liked hospitals, but she let them do an X-ray to see if her ribs were broken—not that there was even much they could do if they were. It turned out two had snapped under the pressure of Phil's blows. It made Erin want to shoot him all over again, especially whenever she looked at Brooke's beautiful face, all bruised and bloodied. She had to remind herself that being alive was the important thing.

Their bodies may have been bruised and beat up, but they were alive and would easily recover—at least physically. Erin knew Brooke's kidnapping and murder of her boyfriend would be difficult to move past, but she also had hope that Brooke was stronger than she had been. This time, Erin was determined to be there for her.

Despite the nurses' protests, Erin had gotten out of her hospital bed and now sat at the foot of Brooke's. She held her hand when they asked questions like, "Will you need a rape kit?"

"No," Brooke quietly murmured, and Erin let out her breath in a rush of relief. Her little sister had been spared the trauma no woman should ever have to endure.

Not long after the nurses left, Janet arrived. She ran straight for Brooke's bed and wrapped her in a tight hug. Erin moved to get up and give them a moment, but then she felt Janet's hand on her arm, pulling her into the embrace with them. Erin was surprised to be included, but for once, she didn't resist.

"My girls," Janet said, crying so hard mascara ran down her face. "Thank God you're okay." She leaned back to look at Erin. "I thought I told you not to put yourself in danger? And then I hear that you ran off—alone!—to some cabin in the woods."

"I also promised to bring Brooke back," Erin said.

Janet's lower lip trembled, and then she sobbed in earnest. "I can't believe I was married to the monster that was responsible for all of this. I let him into our lives! He slept in my bed. He shared the same house as Brooke, and he lied through his teeth, saying he thought of her as his daughter. Like an idiot, I believed him."

"He fooled all of us, Mama," Brooke said, her tone gentle.

"He really was a sociopath," Erin said, placing her hand on Janet's arm. "He could pretend to be normal, but inside, he was completely unhinged."

Janet looked at them both with huge, tearful eyes. "Will you ever be able to forgive me?"

Brooke said yes right away, but to Erin, the question had deeper meaning. It was something therapists had told her countless times, that the only way to truly move on would be to forgive her mother and let go of the pain she carried around like a weight strapped to her chest. But now that she knew the identity of the man who had done this to them, she realized Janet was a victim of Phil's machinations just as much as they were. For the first time in thirteen years, Erin looked at Janet's very real tears and thought, *Yes, I will forgive you.*

"We're all victims of that sick bastard," Erin said, waiting to see what Janet would say. Would she continue to dismiss what happened to Erin when she was seventeen?

Instead, Janet nodded tearfully. "Yes, we all are."

It was a step forward, one that Erin had never expected. Another weight she'd carried around lifted, and hope for the future blossomed within her.

Janet turned her attention to whether Brooke had eaten or not, and Erin left her to fuss over her little sister. She had an apology of her own to make.

She pulled aside the curtain to Adam's bed, and he looked up from his phone. "May I come in?"

He grinned at her. "I like that you're pretending that piece of fabric gives me any privacy, but sure, come in."

She sat down in the uncomfortable armchair by his bed. "I think I owe you an apology."

He raised his eyebrows at her, lifting the bandage on his head where he'd needed a few stitches. "Really?"

"I shouldn't have jumped to conclusions like that and accused you. I was just really upset when I thought you and the other cops cost Brooke her life."

"That's completely understandable. I was furious at them, too."

Her brows furrowed. "What do you mean?"

"They were supposed to wait for my signal, but someone got trigger-happy and sprang the trap too soon."

Erin sat back in surprise. "And that doesn't make you suspicious at all?"

"No, because you were right to worry about the competency of this police force. The sheriff is the worst leader I've ever seen, and these cops haven't had much practice in covert ops like this. You almost can't blame them, except as you said, it almost cost Brooke her life." His face was like granite, his voice tight. "We almost lost both of you because they couldn't wait thirty seconds for my confirmation to come. But at least we can finally do something about this worthless sheriff."

Erin stilled. "What do you mean?"

"I mean once I release all the details of this case to the press and the commissioner, including the fact that your own case was completely ignored seventeen years ago, he won't be sheriff much longer."

"Wow, that's the best news I've heard all day," Erin said, her heart lifting at the thought there might be justice for her after all.

"Should make my life easier, too," Adam said with a half-grin.

"They should make you sheriff. You were the one who made the connection between my case and all the others. If you hadn't ignored Holland and convinced me to come back here, Brooke could have been dead by now. Phil would still be alive and loose, free to take a new girl each year and never stop."

Adam leaned back against his pillow and watched her. "Did you ever suspect it might be Phil?"

"Hell no. I barely knew him, and then when he first stepped out of the shadows, my brain shut down. I couldn't believe what I was seeing."

"I was shocked as hell, too. We investigated him in the beginning as part of due process, but everything with him checked out. History of alcoholism but sober for twenty years. Everyone who worked with him said he was a great boss. Seemed to be an involved dad. No red flags."

Erin shuddered. "He was a sociopath. Appearing normal is what they're good at."

"But he was the one who kidnapped you all those years ago?" When she nodded, he looked away for a moment, hands tight on the sheet of his bed. "It's sick how well he held it together. Even when you were in his house—right in front of him. I'm guessing he looked different back then?"

"He was about half the size, and he always kept that ski mask on." Erin glanced back at their shared hospital curtain and lowered her voice. "Don't feel bad for me, though. It's Brooke I'm worried about. The whole situation was fucked up beyond my wildest dreams."

She told him about the first time she'd met Phil, when he'd approached them after church. "And then at some point after I escaped, he came sniffing around my mom and charmed her into marrying him."

"So they've been living with that son of a bitch for all these years," Adam said with a shake of his head. "Brooke's going to need some serious therapy. Your mom, too."

"Brooke's resilient," Erin said, thinking of how scary that must have been to see Phil choking Erin, but Brooke still tried to save her. She *had* saved her because she'd made it possible to grab the gun.

"Runs in the family," he said with a warm smile. After a moment's hesitation, he asked,

"What will you do now?"

It was a question that had been in the back of her mind the past few hours. "I don't know," she said truthfully. She thought of Janet embracing her along with Brooke and of Brooke's forgiveness for their nonexistent relationship. "Everything is different now. It's all over, finally, after years of the trauma of knowing he was still out there. I just feel so damn relieved to know he's gone. I feel like the part of me that's always been trapped in Huntsville is free now." She glanced at the shared curtain again, where she could just make out the low murmurs of Janet and Brooke talking. "But other aspects of my life are just beginning."

He gave her a knowing look. "You won't be taking the next flight out of here?"

"Well, I wouldn't go that far," she said with a little laugh. "I do have a business I've neglected for days."

"I understand," he said, though he had an expression like he expected something else from her.

Though she felt the beginnings of the first real peace in her heart she'd ever experienced, she knew she couldn't stay here much longer. This wasn't her home anymore, and she had a company that she had to get back to. She planned to stay a few days to make sure Brooke was okay, but then she would return to her life in New York.

She'd had just about as much as she could take of Huntsville.

33

THREE MONTHS LATER

E rin tried to concentrate on the ad design on her screen, but her eyes kept shifting over to her phone to check for messages. Beneath her desk, her leg tapped a steady rhythm.

"Hey, boss lady," Nikki said, leaning in the doorway. "Need any help?"

Erin looked up from her computer gratefully. "No, I'm almost done. Did you find out if the driver picked them up at arrivals?"

Nikki gave a thumbs up. "Everything went smoothly."

"So how much longer until they arrive?"

Nikki checked her watch. "Another twenty minutes or so."

Erin took a deep breath and nodded. "Okay, I can get this knocked out in like five minutes if I can just focus."

"I'll leave you to it, then. Let me know if you need anything."

"Thanks, Nikki," Erin said, already turning back to the monitor.

She found one element of the ad design that wasn't quite right, but when she reached for her pen and notepad, she realized her pen was missing. She still took all her notes on physical paper—she never could get used to using an app to corral her thoughts. With a little huff of frustration, she pulled open her drawer to rummage inside.

Her hand bumped into a pill bottle, and she took it out to examine it. It was one of her half-empty vials of Xanax. She'd kept it at the office in case she ran out of her main supply or just really needed one before she headed home. She stared at the bottle for a moment and was relieved to find that it didn't trigger a need to use any. If anything, all she felt was a twinge of disgust. After everything that happened in Huntsville—literally facing her demons—she'd overcome the daily nightmares and the desperate need for oblivion to escape her thoughts. With satisfying finality, she threw the bottle in the trash.

Her life and mental health may not have been completely perfect, but they were a hell of a lot better than they had been a few months ago. At least she could get on an elevator now without a total nervous breakdown. She would never be able to forget the trauma of her past, but at least she had the strength now to work through it, and she made progress every day.

She finally found a pen, wrote a quick note of things she wanted to change, and then closed out everything on her screen. Just for a moment, she leaned back in her soft leather chair and closed her eyes. Relief that she'd managed to get it all done in time made her feel buoyant.

Her phone rang, and Erin could see it was Nikki's line. She answered with a smile on her face. "Hey, have they gotten here early?"

"Not yet, and I'm so sorry to do this to you now, but Christopher Roland is holding for you."

Erin hung her head down for a second and let out a sigh. "All right. I will have to deal with him sooner or later. May as well be now."

Nikki put him through, and then his overly boisterous voice threatened to blow out her ear drum. "Erin, thank God you're still there! You wouldn't believe—"

"I'm going to have to stop you right there," Erin said, and Christopher made a shocked, choking sound. "I already let you know by phone and email that I'll be out of the office for the next week, and that means I won't be taking any calls or responding to emails. Whatever emergency you're dealing with right now can wait, especially since I know for a fact that the latest campaign is exceeding expectations."

"So this is how you treat one of your oldest clients?" Christopher said, his tone indignant.

"I don't think I've ever once given you something to complain about, so yes, I'm happy to let you know that I'll be taking some much-needed time off. As we've proven to you time and again, my company is the best in the business and you won't be able to find anyone else as devoted and skilled. But you're always welcome to go and find someone else to take over your PR campaign. You know, the one that's currently raking you in millions."

Christopher stuttered out something, clearly shocked at her talking to him like that, but she told him again she'd be back in a week and hung up.

Then she called Nikki, who answered right away. "I put my foot down with Christopher, and it was delicious," Erin said with a huge grin.

"Wow, I'm proud of you! It's about time you stood up to him. I thought he'd blow this place up calling all the time when you were gone."

"That's exactly why I wanted to tell you that all calls from him should be ignored until I come back. And Nikki, I want you to take some time off while I'm gone, too."

Nikki was quiet for a moment. "Okay, who is this?"

Erin laughed. "I'm serious! You work too much. Go live a little."

"Wow, okay, I don't know who you are and what you did with my boss, but I'm just going to pretend you really are Erin because I've honestly heard the beach calling my name for a while now."

"Then consider yourself on vacation starting tomorrow," Erin said. "Now if you'll excuse me, I'm going to go wait in front of the elevators for my special guests to arrive."

"I'm so happy for you, Erin," Nikki said, and she could hear her smiling into the phone.

As Erin walked out of her office, she realized for the first time that this nervous energy she felt—the fluttery feeling in her stomach—was actually from happy excitement for once instead of panic-inducing anxiety. It was a nice change.

The elevator doors pinged cheerfully, and then Janet and Brooke stepped out, both looking around at Erin's floor with awestruck faces. Erin had shown off her company to countless clients, but never before had her heart soared like this.

As soon as Brooke caught sight of Erin, she ran over and threw her arms around her, just like she did when she was little. Erin hugged her back tightly.

"How was the flight?" Erin asked when Janet joined them with a smile.

Erin hugged her mother, too, relieved that she didn't feel any lingering hesitation to show affection. It helped that they'd regularly talked on the phone ever since Erin returned to New York.

"Smooth and fast—couldn't have asked for better," Janet said.

"I'm so excited to be here!" Brooke said, her eyes bright. "New York looks exactly like it does in the movies."

Erin laughed. "We're definitely going to hit all the big tourist sites while you're here."

"Thank you so much for taking Brooke on," Janet said, squeezing Erin around the waist with one arm. "This will be an amazing internship for her."

Brooke would be spending the summer interning at Erin's company to gain experience and help round out her college applications. Erin planned on going with her to check out nearby universities, too.

"I just got my SAT and ACT scores back, and I scored way higher than I expected," Brooke said, beaming.

"That's amazing, Brooke. I'm so impressed that after everything, you focused and finished strong."

Janet smiled at her and gave her a little hug. "I'm so proud of her." She reached over and gave Erin a squeeze. "Of both of you. Look at this place! What an accomplishment."

"Thank you," Erin said, smiling so widely it almost hurt. Looking around her bright, modern office, with her name emblazoned everywhere, she felt even prouder than she had the day she opened for business.

"It's going to be so incredible to come here every day with you," Brooke said with a little squeal.

Erin grabbed hold of her hands and did a happy dance. "We are going to have so much fun."

"It'll be hard to leave you," Janet said, a sad smile on her face. "But I know you girls will have the best time."

"Aw, I'll miss you, Mom. You'll have a whole week to enjoy the city, though," Brooke said.

"How have you been holding up?" Erin asked.

"I've been struggling a bit," Janet admitted with a regretful look. "It's just been really hard knowing that the man I was married to was the one who caused my girls so much suffering."

"He had a lot of people fooled," Erin said as Brooke rubbed her mom's arm.

"Yes, but they didn't live with him," Janet said with a rueful smile. "It's funny that as horrible as he was, I have him to thank for my sobriety. I still attend meetings and keep up with my twelve-step program."

"That's such a relief to hear," Erin said. It was one of the things she'd been afraid of every time she heard Janet sounding down on the phone. Would she regress to her past self-medicating? She was glad she hadn't.

Brooke gave her mother a fond smile. "She's been doing great. I go with her to the meetings sometimes."

"We'll just steer clear of the bars here then," Erin said with a wink, and they laughed. "I have so much planned for this week, your legs will probably give out on you, but we're going to tons of fun doing it."

"Sounds great," Janet said with mock apprehension.

"Today I thought we could do some sightseeing in Manhattan, a little shopping, then dinner and a show. What do you think?"

"Perfection," Brooke said, beaming.

Janet waved her hand toward the big, open space of the lobby. "I hope you plan to give us a tour of your office first."

"Of course! This is my home away from home, so I love to show it off."

She led them toward the design room to start because it was the most fun to look at, with all the gorgeous ad campaigns on display. As they passed the receptionist desk, Nikki intercepted them.

"Erin, I didn't want to interrupt your tour—hi, family!" She said this with a little wave of her arm, bangles jingling merrily. "But there's a call for you that I thought you wouldn't want to miss."

Erin gave her a look. "It better not be Roland."

"No, it's a cop, so I figured when the police call, you should answer."

Erin felt her stomach tighten in a way it hadn't in weeks, but she smiled and nodded so as not to alarm Brooke and Janet. "Okay, I'll take it in my office, then. I was just about to show Brooke and my mother the design room. Could you take over for me for just a minute?"

Nikki did a little salute. "Come along, fam. We're going to go check out the stunning artwork and design this company is famous for."

"I won't be long," Erin promised her sister and mother.

"Take your time," Janet said. "We'll be fine."

In her office, Erin picked up the receiver and pressed the waiting line. "Erin Masters."

"Erin, it's good to hear your voice. This is Adam."

Realizing it was Adam brought a mix of emotions. Happiness warred with apprehension inside her. She thought of Adam as a friend now, but talking to him also brought back some seriously bad memories. Like when he told her Brooke had been kidnapped.

"I'm guessing from that huge silence on your end you're not as happy to hear from me," he said, amusement clear in his tone. "Don't worry, I won't drop a huge bad news bomb on you this time."

She laughed. "I'm sorry, of course I'm glad to talk to you! It's been too long."

"When you didn't call right away after getting back to New York, I figured you needed some time."

"I did promise to call—but I got back here and to my work, and then…" she trailed off, unsure how to say she didn't want regular updates on how the case of the missing girls was going. At least not when she first got back to New York. There was a big part of her that needed to reevaluate her life and decide what was most important. Like cultivating a relationship with Brooke and Janet, not continuing to live in her traumatic past.

"I get it," Adam said, his tone gentle. "I'd want to leave this mess behind, too. I hope you kept up with Brooke and Janet, though."

"They're actually here right now."

"Seriously? That's fantastic! You giving them the grand tour of NYC?"

"Well, I was about to, but then someone interrupted," she said teasingly.

"Oh, I see how it is," he said, and she could picture the smile on his face.

"Brooke and Janet are staying for the week, and then Brooke will be doing an internship at my company for the summer."

"That'll be good for her college applications."

"Definitely. I'm just glad to help her in some way. You know, actually be a supportive big sister."

"I think you always have been, even from afar."

She smiled because Adam really knew how to always say the right thing. "Enough about me. How have you been?"

"A hell of a lot better since Holland got the axe."

Her eyes widened. "He was fired? Seriously?"

"Yes, as soon as word got out that he knew about your kidnapping and did nothing, the commissioner had no choice but to fire him."

"Wow. It's nice to hear there's justice in Huntsville."

"He even admitted why he did that to you."

Erin froze. "What did he say?"

"Apparently, he's always believed his son Rick was responsible—at least in your case and in Brooke's. He never bothered to investigate, so he didn't know about the other girls. He knew Rick was a pedo, had a past relationship with you, and that's why he wouldn't tell you where he lived. The truth was, he didn't know. Guy fell off the map—just another deadbeat dad, I guess."

Hearing for sure that a former sheriff had it out for her just to protect his sick son was more confirmation that Erin and her mother truly had been treated like second-class citizens. "Firing him wasn't enough. I hope he gets run out of town."

"If he does, I probably won't be around to see it."

"What do you mean? Surely this cleared your name and made you a hero!" Thanks to Adam, the families of the missing girls finally had some closure. There hadn't been enough forensic evidence in the basement and the burn pit to connect every missing girl for sure, but there was enough that they knew which girls had likely crossed paths with Phil. And paid the ultimate price.

"Oh it has. They wanted to put my name on the ticket for sheriff, but working with you made me want to look for a big city job again."

"Really? I seem to remember you telling me that Huntsville was growing on you and that you actually liked working in a small town," she said wryly.

He snorted. "That was until I saw that hellhole through your eyes and realized I can't live here with these people."

Erin threw back her head and laughed, thrilled that she had rubbed off on him so intensely. "So where will you go? Back to Chicago?"

"Actually, I applied for a job there. In NYC. My interview is next week."

It took Erin a moment to process what he had said. Adam had been on her mind a lot since leaving Huntsville. He was the reason she was able to finally confront her past and overcome it. He helped save her baby sister. And she'd enjoyed spending time with him in Huntsville—enough that she was surprised to find she missed him when she was back home. That was another reason she hadn't called. She didn't need yet another person pulling her back to Huntsville.

"You are definitely a NYPD-caliber detective. This is fantastic news."

He must have been waiting for her reaction because he immediately said, "How about we grab some drinks and dinner while I'm in town? You could show me around if you can squeeze me into your schedule."

"I would love that," she said truthfully. "And no schedule-squeezing necessary. You coming into town calls for schedule-clearing."

He chuckled, but it sounded relieved. "I'll text you with all the details, okay?"

They said their good-byes, and Erin hung up the phone, knowing she was wearing the biggest smile on her face.

As she returned to her sister and mom, she waited in the doorway of the design room for a moment, just taking in their wide eyes and enthusiastic compliments as Nikki showed them a slideshow of a current campaign. Of course it had to be Christopher Roland's, Erin noted with a little grin to herself.

She thought about the days and weeks ahead, and for the first time in her life, she felt nothing but hopeful anticipation. No anxiety, no guilt, no fear of her past coming back to haunt her.

She was finally free.

NEVER MISS A RELEASE!

Thank you so much for reading THE GIRL WHO GOT AWAY. We hope you enjoyed it!

We have so much more coming your way. Never miss a release by joining our free VIP club. You'll receive all the latest updates on our upcoming books, gain access to exclusive content and giveaways, and get a FREE book!

To sign up, simply visit
www.jackmcsporran.com/download-free-books

Thank you for reading THE GIRL WHO GOT AWAY! If you enjoyed the book, we would greatly appreciate it if you could consider adding a review on your bookstore of choice.

Reviews make a huge difference to the success or failure of a book, especially for writers like us. The more reviews a book has, the more people are likely to take a shot on picking it up. The review need only be a line or two, and it really would make the world of difference for us if you could spare the three minutes it takes to leave one.

With all our thanks,

Jack McSporran & J.A. Leake